IF WE FALL

A WHAT IF NOVEL

NINA LANE

SNOW QUEEN
PUBLISHING

If We Fall
A What If Novel

Published by Snow Queen Publishing

This book is a work of fiction. All names, characters, locations, and incidents are products of the author's imagination, or have been used fictitiously. Any resemblance to actual persons living or dead, locales, or events is entirely coincidental.

Cover photography: Sara Eirew
Cover design: Concierge Literary Designs & Photography

ISBN: 978-1-7360527-1-6

PROLOGUE

Josie

Ten years ago

W here *was* he?

I glanced again at my phone. No message or text. The knot of concern in my chest tightened. It wasn't like Cole not to let me know if he was going to be late. Also, he wouldn't be intentionally late to my parents' surprise twenty-fifth anniversary party, which my sister and I had been planning for months.

Then again, he'd been working overtime finishing classes for his final semester at Ford's College. He also worked three jobs— sternman on a lobster boat, carnival game operator at the Water's Edge Pier, and assistant at the Maine State Aquarium. Most nights he returned to our tiny, cluttered apartment long after I was asleep, then he was gone the next morning before I woke.

We'd been living together for almost a year now, and he

always left me notes and texted me frequently whenever we were apart. But tonight, I hadn't heard from him in over four hours.

That definitely wasn't like him.

Trying to suppress my concern, I slipped my phone back into my purse and rejoined the lively party. "Great Balls of Fire" pounded from the DJ's speaker system, and multicolored balloons accented poster-sized photographs of my parents and the *Happy Anniversary* signs I'd painted. Dozens of family friends and their children enjoyed dancing, plenty of food and drink, and entertainment from a magician, a face painter, and a balloon artist.

"I can't believe you did this." My mother, resplendent in a silk *crepe de Chine* maxi dress embroidered with flowers, appeared at my side. Though I'd followed her artistic career path, she had always possessed a bohemian, stylish flair that I lacked. While I shuffled around in ripped jeans and stained T-shirts, she wore fashionably artistic clothes—Indian-print skirts, patterned scarves, hats.

Even after twenty-five years of marriage, people frequently wondered how Benjamin Mays—tall and handsome, but as conservative as a preacher in his khakis and chambray shirts— had landed the elegantly creative Faith.

The question usually answered itself when people saw how my mother and father looked at each other. Like butter melting on toast. Honey dissolving into hot tea.

"You deserve it." I slipped my arm around her shoulders. "I'm just glad everyone was able to come. Are you all ready for your big anniversary trip to Europe?"

"Yes, thankfully. Your father still has to pack a few things, though." She sipped a glass of champagne, her gaze drifting over the room. "I haven't seen Cole yet. Is he working late?"

My chest tightened. "I think so."

She glanced at me perceptively, a crease appearing between her eyebrows. Not wanting to worry her, I waved to a server who was making the rounds with champagne. "Have another glass and enjoy yourself. I'm going to check on the buffet."

I wove my way through the crowd, pausing to speak briefly with several guests. I retrieved my phone again and stepped outside on to the covered front porch.

Where was he?

Agitated worries pitched and rolled in my head. *He'd gotten tangled in a flying line and was dragged overboard. His battered old Ford had broken down on some isolated road, and he'd been abducted by aliens. He'd gotten lost in the woods. He—*

"Josie!" His deep voice surged against my heart.

My breath caught. I turned, squinting through the dim illumination of the streetlights. He ran toward me, suit jacket flapping open, tie loose around his neck, two bouquets of wildflowers clutched in each hand.

Cole. The boy I had a crush on when I was nine years old. The crush that turned into a wild love.

I hurried to meet him, relief billowing through me. We met halfway down the sidewalk. He extended his arms. I leapt right into them and hugged him hard, pressing my face to his damp hair. The soapy, clean smell of him filled my nose.

"I'm so sorry." He pulled back to look at me, his blue eyes simmering with contained excitement. "We were late getting back, and the catch was incredible which means a much bigger paycheck, but I left my phone on the boat and I was going to come right over but I stank like hell, and then at the docks I ran into Dave Jamison."

I squeezed his hands. "I'm just glad you're okay. Who's Dave Jamison?"

"He's the oceanographer professor visiting from Boston U," Cole explained hastily. "I'd applied for a spot on his research cruise to the Gulf of Mexico. It's privately funded, so it was in high demand and I didn't get in. But he just told me one of his students had to drop out, and he offered me the position. Two weeks. We'll be able to test the microbial sampler *on the sea floor.*"

His face lit up like he'd just told me they would be raising a pirate's treasure chest from the deep. I smiled. My concern slipped away, replaced by happiness and pride that all his hard work would be rewarded. Not wanting to use his father's money, Cole had put himself through five years of the undergrad Marine Sciences program at Ford's. A spot on a prestigious research cruise would not only enhance his credentials and future opportunities but allow him to do the work he loved.

"That's amazing." I slid my arms around his waist and stood on tiptoe to kiss him. My entire being filled with the light and heat we generated so quickly. "Congratulations. No one deserves a spot on that cruise more than you."

"I'm sorry I'm so late." Shifting the two flower bouquets to one hand, he finger-combed his damp hair and attempted to smooth the wrinkles from his shirt. "Do I look okay?"

Okay was an understatement for Cole Danforth's appearance. Tall and muscular with sun-streaked brown hair and thick-lashed blue eyes, his skin tanned golden-brown…my guy was as tempting and delicious as warm cinnamon toast.

"You look incredible," I assured him.

He extended a bouquet of wildflowers to me and knotted his tie. We returned to the party, where he gave my mother the second bouquet and whispered something that made her smile and hug him with boundless affection.

"What'd you say to Mom?" I asked him, after he'd gone to talk to my father and twelve-year-old brother Teddy and we were heading to the dance floor.

"I told her I was looking forward to the day you and I get to celebrate our twenty-fifth anniversary." He winked at me.

"Oh my *God.*" I pressed a hand to my chest. Every age my heart had been—eight, eleven, nineteen—came together in one swelling, happy beat, a chorus of song. "I have loved you forever, Colton Danforth."

"Can I get a picture of you guys?" Teddy approached us, his digital camera in his hands, and a cake pop stuck behind his ear. For safekeeping, I assumed.

Cole wrapped his arm around my shoulders, pulling me into his side as we smiled through several snaps of the shutter. The celebration continued on a wave of happiness. When the clock approached one, my father signaled to me that it was time for him and my mother to leave.

"Come with us." I tugged Cole's hand as we walked to the foyer. "I came over with Mom, Dad, and Teddy. I'm sleeping at their house tonight so I can drive them to the airport tomorrow morning. Teddy's coming too. We can drop them off and go out for breakfast."

"Waffle Castle?" Cole asked hopefully.

"Yes! Butter Pecan Special for the win!" Teddy gave a fist pump as he skirted past us, balancing a white bakery box in one hand.

A flurry of activity followed as we pulled on our jackets, gathered our belongings, and said goodbye to the guests who had followed us to the door. Teddy's camera continued to flash on and off.

"Last picture, Mom and Dad!" he shouted at our parents.

"I'll take one of you all." Cole held out his hand for the camera and gestured for me to join my parents. "Vanessa, over here."

My older sister and I stood on either side of our parents, our arms entwined and my mother holding the wildflower bouquets Cole had given me and her. Teddy posed in front of us, pointing gleefully to the bakery box, which must have held leftover cake.

After the camera flashed, my parents eased away to say final goodbyes to a few well-wishers. Teddy opened the bakery box and scooped out a fingerful of cake.

I picked up my purse and glanced toward my parents. They

stood alone near the coatrack. My father rested his hand on my mother's cheek. They gazed at each other with expressions of such tender devotion that my heart skipped a beat.

Would Cole and I be the same way in twenty-five years? Would we have children and celebrations filled with friends and laughter? Would we still hold hands, steal kisses, exchange secret smiles?

I wished for the answer to be a resounding *yes*.

As I started past him to the door, he stopped me with his arm and bent to press his lips swiftly against mine. I absorbed the warm kiss, his salt-and-citrus scent, the light rasp of his stubble. My soul fluttered with love, happiness, and the tiny but ever-present fear that we were too fortunate, it was too good, we were too young. Everything about us was too perfect.

"Come on, Josie Bird." Cole lifted his head and placed his hand on my lower back, guiding me to the door. "Let's fly."

What if I had known it would be our last kiss?

What if I had known how hard we would fall?

CHAPTER 1

Josie

Present

I can't find my flashlight.

Dread creeps up my spine, intensifying my sweaty-palmed anxiety. I turn on the second interior car light and rummage through my black backpack again for my 3100 lumens, quad core LED, rechargeable aluminum Fenix U52 Cree flashlight with its beautiful 276 yards of throw. I always keep it in the side pocket for easy access, but right now—when I need it the most—I can't find it.

I pull in a heavy breath. I shouldn't have driven myself here from the train station, but the train from Boston had been late and all the cabs gone. I'd had to choose between renting a car or spending the night alone at the station. I might've made the wrong choice.

The combination of driving and darkness has ratcheted my

stress to new levels. Plus four days of cross-country travel from California to Maine on trains and buses, not to mention more lack of sleep than usual, are taking their toll. My eyes are peppery with fatigue, my muscles ache, and I'm struggling not to be entirely freaked out about returning to my hometown for the first time in ten years.

Though I've told myself I need to confront my phobias, I didn't mean *all at the same time.*

I unzip the main pocket of the backpack, pushing aside my clothes, toiletries bag, and a book to reach the bottom. Nothing. For the third time, I search the other pockets, though the growing dismay in my stomach tells me I'm not going to find it.

Getting to my knees, I squeeze over the console to reach my art case in the backseat. I haven't opened the case once during my trip, but I search it anyway. Nothing except watercolors, pencils, pastels, and charcoal.

With a groan, I shove open the door and step into the late June night. Cold salty air rushes against my face, stilling me for an instant. I've lived in San Francisco for almost a decade and the smell of the ocean is nothing new, but *this* is the Atlantic. This is lobster, fried dough, fireflies. This is splintered old picnic tables, sunburned noses, blueberries.

This is—

I slice through that thought before it has a chance to form. I bend to feel the floor of the rental car. Nothing. My travel bag in the trunk only has more clothes and my sleeping bag.

Dammit.

After slamming the trunk, I zip up my old army jacket. The small circular parking lot, empty aside from my car, only has one light casting a yellowish tinge over the pavement. Heavy coastal fog obscures the moon.

I squint at the cove, a half-circle of black water. Pallid dock lights cast shadows on the fishing boats and the hulking shapes of the warehouses.

On the opposite side at the Water's Edge Pier, brighter lights illuminate the restaurants, souvenir shops, and pubs. At the end of the pier, the colorful Ferris wheel spins, twinkling merrily, the carousel and smaller carnival rides clustered at the base. It's a welcoming sight, promising noise, people, lights—all the things that scare away whatever lurks in the dark.

If I can make my way to the pier, I can buy another flashlight at one of the shops. It won't be anything like my Fenix Cree, but at least it will provide me with *some* light.

I tighten my grip on the open door. The stretch of beach between my car and the pier is shadowy and badly lit. I'm parked at the end of the road. The only way to drive to the pier from here is to take the isolated two-lane road around town. Which means more driving in the dark. I'd managed to get here from the train station without having a panic attack, but I'm inching closer to the edge.

To my right, the southern hill is nothing but an endless swath of black. I can't see the cottage at the top of the path, the towering pines that shelter it in a half-circle.

I can picture it, though. Lopsided and odd, Watercolor Cottage is the only building on the steeply graded slope of the southern hill—all the other proper houses having had the good sense to be constructed on the flatter land near downtown Castille.

By contrast, my mother's former studio, still in defiance of all good architectural planning, is latched to the hill like a barnacle. My father had intended to build the house to align with the landscape, but—knowing nothing about either house-building or landscaping—he made it up as he went along. And so the cottage became a mishmash of weird angles, sloped ceilings, misshapen doorways, and floors that tilt downhill.

My mother had loved it madly. The cottage had been her escape, the place she went when she needed to work in solitude. Now I need to do the same thing there.

I haven't been to the cottage in well over ten years. It's a quarter-mile hike up the hill, and I can't even start walking without a flashlight.

A chill prickles my skin. I get back in the car and slam the door. The pale stream of the headlights reaches the edge of the beach before dissolving.

Through the windshield, I see the silhouette of a tall man walking from the docks lining the harbor. I watch him for a second before realizing he's coming toward my car.

Probably a police officer patrolling the harbor who thinks he's about to catch a couple of kids making out.

Or not.

I lock the doors. The headlights catch a pair of large black shoes, distinctly male. He walks with a long, steady stride, each step certain, like he knows his way around here. He's wearing dark trousers and a black jacket open to reveal a suit and tie. Not a cop's uniform. I should get out of here.

Just as I reach for the key, a sudden familiarity bolts through me. I know that walk. That body. That—

No.

Before he steps fully into the glow of the headlights, I look away. My hand shakes as I start the ignition. Then his knuckles rap on the glass of the driver's side window. My breath sticks in my throat. I don't know what to do.

What if I'm wrong? What if it's not him?

Or...maybe worse...*what if it is?*

Wary, I glance out the window. He steps away from the car. The overhead light illuminates his face. Our eyes meet with a charge so strong that time both dissolves and expands in the same instant.

Oh my God.

Everything inside me goes haywire, a thousand electrical currents crossing and sparking. He's older, his strong features set in hard lines that make him look almost like a stranger, but even across the distance, one look at his thick-lashed eyes tells me the truth.

This formidable man is Cole Danforth, my first love. My *only* love—back when I believed in things like love and wishes coming true.

And long before he shattered my heart into a million pieces and ground them beneath the heel of his work boot.

His eyes widen. For an instant, I wonder how he knows it's me, but then I remember the interior car lights are on.

I press a hand to my chest. My heart is a hammer pounding at my ribs. Though I'd known when I decided to return to Castille, I'd have to see him again one of these days, I hadn't expected it to be so soon. Right *now*.

He's tall and imposing, broad in the shoulders, but the lines of his body are devoid of the warm approachability that was such an intrinsic part of the boy I once loved.

His mouth shapes one word. *"Josie."*

My heart hitches. Heat blooms through me. I can almost feel his lips against my skin, the sound of my name in his hoarse, sexy groan.

Oh no. For ten years, I've not only been unable to *forget* all the things he could do to me, I've thought about them in shocking, vivid detail. And there is no way in hell I can let him sense that, especially five seconds after seeing him again.

"Cole." His name comes out on a breath only I can hear. I can't remember the last time I said his name aloud.

Despite everything, it's still the most delicious name I've ever spoken, one that tastes like everything good. Powdered sugar, ripe berries, ice cream. It's the only name I've ever whispered with love, snapped in anger, cried out in lust. It's the only name I ever wrote on a school folder, linked to mine with the eternal plus sign. *Josie + Cole.*

He indicates I should roll down the window. My hand shaking, I press the button.

Silence floods the space between us, borne on the salt-drenched fog that carries countless shared memories. He approaches slowly and bends to peer into the open window. My blood quickens, like his presence is the flare of a match and I'm the candle.

"What are you doing here?" His tone is clipped, not a trace of surprise or pleasure.

I swallow to ease my dry throat. "Hello to you too. Didn't… didn't you know I was coming back?"

"No."

"I'm here until the middle of August," I explain. "I'm going to paint a mural in Lantern Square."

"A mural?"

"It's a large painting done directly on a wall."

"I know what it is. Why are you painting one?"

My shoulders tighten. *Because I have to. Because it's the tenth year of my parents' deaths, and the mural should have been completed years ago.*

Six months after the fatal car crash, the Castille Historical Society had proposed the mural in honor of my parents. My mother had been a prominent local artist, and my father had served as the Historical Society president for over twenty years. He'd penned several books about the history of Castille, and both my parents were frequently involved with local fundraisers, charities, and festivals.

My sister and I had both moved out of Castille by the time the Society brought the proposal to the city council. Then the town was hit with an economic downturn, and the proposal got lost in the shuffle. Maybe that had been a blessing in disguise. I'm not sure I could have come back so soon, if the project had gone through then.

But now? I need to paint something *new*. Before the accident, my art had been populated by fairytale creatures and animals in magical settings inspired by storybooks. Lamp-lit forests, cobblestone streets, old libraries, lively taverns, toppling cottages. Barefoot girls with lighted candles had often made their way through the intricate landscapes in search of...*something*.

In the decade since the accident, my art has grown increasingly dark, the weird, whimsical creatures and long-haired girls taken over by phobias and nightmares. I painted my most recent series, *Distortion*, in the midst of mind-numbing insomnia that brought horrific images to mind—ghastly, disfigured human and animal faces peering through chaotic darkness, skin peeling off, eyes vacant black holes.

They scared the shit out of me. They'd also sold out three months ago at a gallery exhibition that had been my breaking point. I realized this manifestation of my torture, the gaping, sightless, skeletal faces, would continue to live on. Invading other people's homes.

Panic hit me so hard I'd been unable to breathe. Only when I came out of it did the knowledge click into place.

I need to go back home. To do something for my parents and make peace with the past. To banish my demons instead of letting them scare me. I need an entirely new inspiration and focus for my art. Something big, expansive, positive, beautiful.

Not that I could ever explain any of that to Cole.

"I offered to paint a mural about the history of Castille," I tell him. "Allegra King and the city council agreed it would be a great way to celebrate the town's Bicentennial Festival in August, so they approved my proposal."

A muscle ticks in his clenched jaw. "And why are you sitting out here?"

Good question. I'm not about to tell him I'm stuck in a running car with all the lights on because I'm too fucking scared to face the dark without my security flashlight.

"I'm enjoying the view," I say.

"Josie." The word snaps out of him, irritated and hard.

What the fuck right does he have to be annoyed that I'm back? He's

the one who walked away from me. He's the one who gave up on us. I'm
the one who has the right to be pissed off.

I can't say any of that aloud, can't dredge up the black, torturous quicksand in which we'd been mired. Not because I care about him, but because I don't want to reopen *my* old wounds that will never fully heal.

"I just got in from the train station." I jerk my thumb toward the southern hill. "I'm staying at my mother's cottage."

"Why aren't you staying with your sister?"

I flex my hands on the steering wheel, trying to ignore the pang in my heart. "I need the quiet and space to work, both on the mural and my other art. I was supposed to get in next week, but I left sooner than I'd expected. I just took the last train in from Boston. Vanessa hasn't responded to my text yet."

Cole pushes back from the window. "So you want to get out of the car?"

"No, actually, I'm good here."

He expels a breath of frustration. "Get out, Josie."

"Go away, Cole."

"You can't just sit here alone." He yanks open the car door. "It's not safe."

Despite my rebellious urge not to obey, I do have to get out of the damned car at some point or I'll end up sitting here for the rest of the night.

I also don't want him to know I'm on the verge of being a total hot mess. He's the only one who's ever seen me stripped bare, utterly defenseless, wrecked. I'll never let him see me the slightest bit vulnerable again.

I turn off the engine, grab my backpack, and get out of the car. Though he's stepped away from me, his presence elicits a ripple of awareness. And unease.

"Come on." He jerks his chin toward the hill. "I'll walk you up."

I'm not sure which would be worse—climbing the dark hill

with Cole or *without* a flashlight. Not that I'm capable of doing either one.

I make a show of looking at my watch. "I'm going over to the pier first. I need to pick up a few things." *Like a massive industrial-sized flashlight.*

"I'm heading back there too."

Great. Now I have to pretend like I'm not scared shitless, even with the dock lights providing some illumination.

Gathering a breath, I start toward the pier. He falls into step beside me, matching his longer stride to mine as if nothing has changed.

I walk faster. I'd known when I decided to come back to Castille that memories would crash and roll through me like a tsunami. I wouldn't be able to make sense of them—bittersweet, torturous, happy, unbearable—but I thought I'd have time to process them before seeing Cole again. Instead his proximity, the movement of his body that had once been so familiar to me, elicits a pain so sharp I feel it to my bones.

"What are you doing out here at this time of night?" I ask.

"There's an event over at the Ivy. I was taking a walk. Needed a break."

I glance in the direction of the upscale restaurant located on its own pier at the north end of the cove. That explains Cole's tailored suit.

"What kind of event?"

"Wedding reception."

"Yours?" I ask before I can stop myself.

His mouth twists. "A colleague's."

He offers no further information. Despite the chilly ocean air, embarrassment heats my face. *Fishing much, Josie? Why? Because you want to know if Cole found happiness with someone else? So what if he did?*

My breath shortens. It would piss me off if he did. Though resentment is the only feeling I have left for him, it would make me sick to think he'd destroyed what we had only to find it again with another woman.

While I, on the other hand, have deliberately sabotaged several relationships with perfectly nice men over the past decade because they didn't give me what Cole and I had had. Yet another reason to resent both him and the ghost of *us* that has never stopped haunting me.

I quicken my pace again, following the dock toward the bright pier lights. Music drifts on the ocean air, and happy screams from the carnival riders float toward the stars. It's close to eleven, and the families have all headed home, leaving older and more boisterous revelers.

As we step onto the wooden pier, the sensory overload—the smell of fried clams, the pinging from the arcade games, Elvis's liquid tones, the flashing neon signs—sharpens the jagged break between my past and present.

I divert into a souvenir shop cluttered with T-shirts, keychains, and tote bags. At the front counter, plastic bins hold toys and knickknacks.

I grab a handheld flashlight with a camouflage design, weighing it in my hand. It's not great, maybe 120 lumens max, but it's likely the best I'll find at a pier shop. I bring it to the register.

"We have these with the Castille logo and lighthouse on the side." The girl behind the counter indicates another basket of flashlights. "If you want one as a souvenir."

"No, that's okay." I dig into my backpack for my wallet. "I grew up here, actually."

"Yeah?" She rings up the flashlight. "Where do you live now?"

"California. San Francisco."

"Oh, cool." She takes my ten and hands me the flashlight and my change. "Welcome home."

Home.

Home should be bright, colorful, happy. It's not. But many of my memories are, which is what I need to focus on. For the first time in ten years, I have important reasons to be back in Castille —to both honor my parents and to be there for my sister during the last few months of her pregnancy. Not even Cole Danforth can divert me from my purpose.

I thank the salesgirl and slip the flashlight into the side pocket of my backpack. Cole is looking at a shelf of books by local authors. On a shelf not blocked by his body, prominently displayed facing outward, are several books about Castille's history by Benjamin Mays.

An ache radiates through my jaw. Tears sting my eyes. I blink them away and shift my gaze to Cole. Now that I can see him more clearly in the light, the shock of his physicality hits me for the first time.

He's even taller than I remember, well over six feet, his black jacket stretching over his broad back and shoulders. His long legs, clad in dark, expensive-looking trousers, are planted solidly apart, like he's securing the earth with his stance.

As if sensing my gaze, he turns and starts toward me. My breath catches. All I can do is stare at him, his long-legged stride eating up the distance between us in both space and time. His dark brown hair is shorter, a neat businessman's style, no longer streaked with gold from the sun. Beneath a tailored gray suit jacket, his white dress shirt stretches across a wide chest that looks as if it's carved of granite.

Good God. I'd watched him grow up, and when we started dating when I was nineteen years old, I'd considered him a man. He'd been in his last year of college, worked two jobs to support himself, and did all the adult things that I, just ending my freshman year, had yet to experience.

But now he's taken the word *man* to a whole new level. Even his features have changed, the angles now lined with a hardness that hadn't been there before. His thick-lashed blue eyes are shuttered, his jaw covered with stubble, his beautiful mouth—his *mouth* that used to do such lovely, dirty things to my body —compressed.

I edge toward the door, suddenly self-conscious in my old army jacket and torn jeans, my hair a rat's nest falling to my shoulders. I'm not sure my system can withstand both seeing him again so unexpectedly and processing the sheer masculine beauty of what he's become.

He moves past me to grab the door handle. His scent fills my nose—expensive things like leather, bergamot, and sandalwood. A polar opposite to the way he used to smell. Back then, it was boat oil and salt water, underscored by the citrus notes of his shaving cream and the secret, delicious essence that belonged to him alone.

I'm lying on our bed, our legs entangled, the sheets twisted around our bodies. The sweet smell of an orange fills the air. He turns the fruit over in his palm, peeling away the skin and separating it into sections with his long fingers. He holds a juicy slice out and slides it into my mouth, brushing his thumb against my lips...

I block the image before it can go any further.

This imposing, suited-up man is not the Cole I once knew and loved. He's no longer the wary, suspicious boy I'd seen in the woods on the way to school. The troubled teenager who'd been the target of unpleasant gossip. The striking young man who'd been making his own way in college.

His gaze slips to the ragged black backpack I'm holding. Something flashes in his eyes that I can't quite define or grasp. Like a fleeting glimpse of sorrow.

Then it's gone so fast I'm not sure it was there at all.

He pulls the shop door open for me.

"Thank you." I step back onto the pier.

"You're welcome."

The stiff formality between us grates on my nerves. The last time we saw each other, we'd both been crying so hard we could barely breathe. We were raw, flayed open, ripped apart. It's difficult to believe this remote man was once the shattered boy who hauled me against his heaving chest and pressed his tear-streaked face into my hair before walking out of my life.

I force the memory away, knowing it will never disappear. I've learned to control my memories when I'm awake, keep them at bay, but on the rare moments when sleep traps me, they burst to the surface like pockets of lava, hot and blistering. Those last few minutes with Cole are the most frequent, the final searing rip between before and after.

How often does he think of that day? Of the time before?

He steps onto the pier behind me. "What else do you need?"

"Nothing."

He lifts an eyebrow. "You only needed a flashlight?"

"Yes. Thanks for your help. I—"

Jingling calliope music suddenly fills the air, the automated, happy sound of bells and a pipe organ. At the end of the pier, the Ocean Carousel starts to spin. A few laughing teenagers cling to the bobbing sharks and tropical fish. Lights flash and glow, illuminating the entire ride like a constellation.

I picture Cole and me...eleven years ago, both of us astride that ridiculous grinning whale, his arm firm around my waist.

I risk a glance at him. He's standing a few feet away, his hands in his pockets and his expression closed. Not a single emotion flickers in his eyes, as if he's hardened on the inside as much as he has on the outside.

"I need to go." I start toward the beach again and turn on the flashlight.

"I'll walk you up to the cottage."

My back teeth come together. It used to be like that. Cole's *I* statements were always exactly that—statements, not questions. He'd never say, "Can I walk you up?" or "Do you need me to go with you?" When he said he was doing something, that meant *he was doing it.*

Apparently that hasn't changed.

"No." I stop and face him. "I'm going alone."

He frowns. "It's not safe."

You're not safe.

As scared as I am of the dark, I'm much more scared of being alone with Cole. Of being anywhere near him again.

"You don't get to protect me anymore." I back away, both hands up like I'm trying to ward him off. "You lost that right when you..."

...broke up with me? "Breaking up" doesn't begin to convey what happened between us. The words don't exist to describe our last encounter.

His jaw tightens. "As a courtesy, I'll walk you up to the cottage."

"I don't need your courtesy or chivalry," I snap. "I don't need anything from you anymore."

I turn and flee, hurrying toward the beach. My breath burns my chest. I half-expect to hear his heavy footsteps behind me, but then the gloom of the harbor encloses me. My ears fill with the roar of dread.

Somehow, I manage to get back to my car. I'll get my suitcase and art portfolio tomorrow morning; the more I drag up the hill, the harder it will be. I have enough clothes in my backpack for the night.

Impenetrable shadows cloak the path leading up to the cottage. The souvenir shop flashlight barely cuts a swathe through the blackness. My heart thunders. I glance back toward the pier. It's too far away to see if Cole followed me to the docks.

Not that I want him to. It's either the dark of the hill or the dark of Cole Danforth. At least I have a flashlight to battle the hill. Aside from rage and pain, I have no weapons against Cole.

I turn and plunge into the dark.

CHAPTER 2

Josie

I can't see. *A demon is chasing me.*

I stumble up the hill, my sneakers slipping on rocks and holes. My breath scrapes my throat. Shadows close in on me from all sides, heavy and suffocating.

Making it worse, as always, is the voice in the back of my mind, taunting and shrill.

Coward. Fucking woman up, Josie, and stop being such a baby. There are a thousand worse things to be scared of than lack of light.

Shut up, I snap back. The voice wasn't there when darkness flooded my life, my brain. When it obliterated my consciousness and part of my memory.

It doesn't know that everything bad happens in the dark.

Countless times as a kid, I'd climbed this hill, had once known every groove in the earth. I latch on to a memory of bursting through the door of Watercolor Cottage, inhaling the smells of clay and oil paint. My mother coming in from the sunroom, her hair pulled back by a bandanna, her smile wide and welcoming.

The image splinters, then explodes into a million pieces. Fear chokes me, pounds in my blood. Fixing my focus downward, I concentrate on the pale light of the flashlight.

Follow it. Follow the path.

I force myself to walk slowly, fighting the urge to run despite the prickling sensation that something is chasing me.

Nothing is chasing you, the voice sneers.

Bullshit. The past is always hovering, poised to lunge and swoop down on me like a sharp-taloned death eater.

I put one foot in front of the other, again and again. Blessedly, the light shines on a worn gray flagstone. Then another. The stones lead to the front door of the cottage, curved like the entrance to a hobbit hole.

Fumbling for the key, I shine the light on the door handle. My hand shakes violently, but I manage to insert the key into the lock and turn it. The door clicks.

Thank God.

Swallowing a gasp, I stagger into the house and feel for the light switches on the wall. I shove all three switches upward, desperate for the explosion of light to ground me, ease my panic, show me where the hell I am.

Nothing happens.

Oh fuck no.

My breath gets faster. I flip the switches again and again, but the cottage remains dark, clouded in murky shadows, filled with terror.

Disembodied heads, skinless and skeletal, loom through the blackness, mouths agape, eyes empty sockets with burning pinpoints of red. The ghastly creatures who have haunted me for a decade.

Stay calm. Get to the sunroom, the kitchen. There are more lights.

Bracing my hand on the wall, I make my way to the sunroom with the big picture window overlooking the cove. I find a floor lamp and pull the chain. It's dead. I try the lights in the kitchen, even knowing before I flip the switch that nothing will break the suffocating darkness. All I have is a thin souvenir shop flashlight, which for me is like going into war with only a needle as a weapon.

Shit. Pressing a hand to the wall, I drag air into my tight lungs. I can't make it back down the hill. I can't stay here either. I'll go crazy.

You are crazy. What kind of adult woman is so scared of the dark she can't even sleep for fear she won't wake up?

This one.

I drop my backpack and sink to the floor, pulling my knees to my chest, my grip so tight on the flashlight my fingers ache. Painful gasps saw from my chest.

"Josie."

His voice is a sudden stream of gold slicing through the dark. My chest tightens. I'm imagining it, an unexpected memory pushing through the fear, breaking my defenses. Once upon a time, nothing was of more comfort to me than Cole's voice. I'd heard it even in the wrenching torture of heartbreak.

But then the broad silhouette of his body is kneeling in front of me. His hands close on my shoulders, a heavy, solid weight easing me away from the knife's edge of panic. I angle the flashlight on his face—the hard set of his features, the burning concern in his eyes, the slash of his mouth.

"Can you stand up?" he asks.

I manage to nod, clawing one hand around his arm. Part of my brain registers the fact that he didn't ask the obvious question, *"What's wrong?"*

Because he already knows. He's the only one who ever will.

I pull myself to my feet. He picks up my backpack and puts his arm around my shoulders. I stiffen, resisting the contact of his body with mine, but his grip tightens. Again, it's either him or the dark.

This time, I choose him. He guides me to the door.

The chilly night air washes over my hot face. I'm still shaking so hard my bones rattle, but blindly I let Cole lead the way back down the hill, his footsteps secure and certain, the solidness of his body and weight of his arm an unexpectedly welcome relief.

"D-don't you want my flashlight?" I ask through chattering teeth. "You can't see anything."

"It's easy once you know the way."

The comment brushes against a deep part of my memory, but I can't shape it into anything meaningful.

We reach the parking lot. He pulls open the passenger side door of my car and urges me inside. Clutching the flashlight, I climb into the seat. Though the light is still dim, at least I can see better now. My breath eases.

Cole gets into the driver's seat and slams the door, rummaging through my backpack for the keys. I press my hands to my eyes and gulp back a sob. So much for *I'll never let him see me vulnerable again.*

"I'll take you to your sister's." He shoves the key into the ignition.

"No." I lower my hands. "She's visiting a friend in Portland through the weekend. I don't have a key to the house or the alarm code. She wasn't expecting me until the end of next week, and I didn't know she hadn't gotten the cottage ready yet. Hold on."

I take my phone from my backpack and swipe the screen. No response from Vanessa.

"She probably won't get my text until morning."

"You talk to her much?" Cole shoves the gear shift into reverse.

"No." Old regret mixes with my lingering panic. "But that's part of the reason I came back. She's pregnant."

"I heard." After guiding the car out of the parking lot, he heads onto a two-lane coastal road leading away from town. I can't bring myself to turn off the stupid flashlight. He hasn't turned off the car's interior lights either.

"She's due in early September." I fiddle with the strap on my backpack, not sure why I'm telling him this. "Her husband ran out on her. That's why she moved back to Castille. I'd have been here sooner, but I had a job I needed to finish."

Cole frowns. "So you came back for your sister."

"Partly, yes." I stare at my pale reflection in the window. "I'd been thinking about the mural for a while, and then when Vanessa moved back, it seemed like the perfect time."

He glances at me. "Why did you offer to paint the mural?"

"In honor of my parents."

His eyes flash with shock. Brief, but unmistakable.

Silence floods the space between us before he pulls up beside a wrought-iron gate situated within a high brick wall. He rolls down the window and punches an access code into an electronic panel. The gate opens, allowing him to navigate a driveway to an oceanfront mansion and cultivated gardens illuminated by floodlights.

"W-where are we?" I stammer.

"My house." He cuts off the engine and grabs my backpack.

Questions push past my exhaustion, but I can't process any of them. I follow him out of the car. He takes my suitcase from the trunk and heads to the front door, pushing a series of buttons on another electronic panel.

Light explodes everywhere. Flooding the porch, filling the tiled foyer, seeping from the multiple rooms. I register the airy, beautiful interior—a curving staircase leading to the upstairs floors, crown molding, wall sconces, an inlaid marble floor.

He leads me to the kitchen, an expansive space of warm maple cabinets and quartz countertops, with a window looking out to a lighted pool surrounded by a rock garden and waterfall.

"When did you move in here?" I can't quite believe he lives in this place, but looking at him in his expensive suit and tie...

"I bought it a few years ago." He takes two bottles of water from the refrigerator and cracks one open before handing it to me.

"You've been back in Castille for that long?"

"Eight years." He tilts his head back to swallow some water. My gaze shifts involuntarily to the movement of his strong throat. "I moved back when my father was diagnosed with lung cancer."

Though his voice is flat, I sense all the emotions simmering underneath that statement. Kevin Danforth had been publicly admired and popular, but in private he'd been a horrible, abusive man. Cole had despised him. Even now, I can't believe he'd have returned to nurse his father during his illness.

"I'm sorry." I don't know what else to say. "I didn't know."

He shrugs as if it doesn't matter. A muscle ticks in his jaw. "I bought the Iron Horse shortly after he was diagnosed. He died not long after that."

Shocked, I lift my head to stare at him. "You own his brewery now?"

"No. I shut it down. I own a company I started after I left Castille. Invicta Spirits. We produce a number of brands of distilled liquor."

Confusion knots my chest. Back when we were together, Cole had been determined to break away from his father and everything Kevin Danforth stood for. He'd hated his father's company, the brewery, even the smell of beer. He'd been all about the ocean, working out on the water in the heat of the sun.

And now he owns a liquor company? Based on this house alone, obviously he's been hugely successful, but I don't understand how or why he took such a path. I'm not sure I want to know either. We both changed drastically after what we endured —how could we not? But to think he's also become a completely different person *on the inside* than the boy I once loved so wildly...

I grip the water bottle in both hands. I hadn't expected any of this. I'd hoped I could just avoid him. Now, already, too many old emotions are pushing at the armor I locked around my heart the day he left me.

Cole sets his water down and bends to pick up a slender cat that I hadn't seen enter the room. Spindly with a tufted gray coat and comically large ears, the cat butts his head against Cole's hand. He obliges by scratching the animal under the chin.

For the first time, his demeanor is unguarded, his features even softening slightly. A sudden litany of questions bubble into my mind.

Do you still like navigating by the stars? Do you still fold your pizza before you eat it? Do you still watch The Three Stooges and eat your sugary breakfast cereal while standing by the sink?

Another image rises, but slowly this time, like a treasure coming to the surface of a lake.

Cole is bare-chested and wearing only a pair of loose drawstring pajama pants, with a bowl of Lucky Charms cupped in one hand. He's leaning back against the kitchen counter, the sun falling through the window behind him and burnishing the smooth muscles of his back.

I stop in the doorway, drinking in the sight of his sleep-rumpled hair, the half-moon nail marks I'd left on his shoulders last night, the ladder-like ridges of his abdomen and the dark trail of hair disappearing beneath his waistband.

He looks up and catches my eye. The warm smile that blooms on his face electrifies me with love and lust. I cross the room to fold myself against him, and our lips meet in a kiss that softens every part of me.

A shiver courses unexpectedly down my spine. My hostility toward Cole, rather to my chagrin, has never eradicated the memory of our sex life. Of *him*. I'd lost my virginity to him, and the hot, fulfilling encounter had set the stage for our future physical relationship.

Young and eager, we'd done everything together. He knew every inch of my body, all the sweet spots that made me tingle, all the right places to touch me. He'd fit inside me with smooth, easy perfection.

Even with my insomnia and nightmares, my subconscious hasn't forgotten. On rare occasions, an erotic dream has made its way into my broken sleep—our naked bodies rubbing together, our lips clinging, open and hot.

And my outright *fantasies…*

Heat flushes my cheeks. I've never been able to reconcile my resentment with the explicit images of him, of us, that I've indulged in over the years. But given the darkness of the rest of my life, I figure I'm entitled to a bit of raw heat every now and then. Even if I'm still alone.

Especially if I'm alone.

Clearing my throat, I refocus on the cat Cole is still holding. "What's his name?"

"Curly. Found him down by the docks a couple of years ago." He sets the cat down and picks up my luggage. "You can sleep in one of the guest rooms tonight."

Aside from the fact that it would be rude to refuse, I have no strength left. I certainly can't drive myself anywhere else tonight.

I follow him up the winding staircase to a lovely room with cream-colored walls and a white four-poster bed covered with a fluffy peach comforter and pillows.

Surely he doesn't live here alone. The thought twists inside me like a corkscrew.

"Bathroom's through that door." Cole puts my ratty old suitcase and backpack on a polished wooden trunk at the foot of the bed. "Where's your cell?"

I take my phone out of my backpack.

"Put my number in." He rattles off his phone number. "Text me so I have yours. I'm on the next floor up."

After texting him with my number, I place the phone on the

antique nightstand. Though I loathe having to ask, my need for the truth outweighs my embarrassment.

"Do you live here alone?"

"Yes." He pushes back his cuff, which glints with a silver cuff-link. Wrapped around his strong wrist is a leather watch with a gold-edged face that looks like one of those ridiculously priced European brands I've seen on wealthy art collectors.

"I'll call a contractor, tell him to go to the cottage tomorrow morning," he says. "He'll get the electricity working and do whatever other repairs are needed. I'll text you when he's done."

Resistance stiffens my spine. I don't want to be indebted to Cole for anything, least of all repairs to my mother's old cottage.

"It's not for you." As if sensing my urge to protest, he lifts a hand. "I don't want you staying here any longer than necessary."

Pressing my lips together, I try to deflect a stab of pain. I don't want to stay here even one night, so his remark shouldn't hurt. But it does.

"You can take the key," I reply shortly. "I have a spare. I should be able to reach Vanessa tomorrow. If the repairs can't get done, I'll figure out a way to stay at her house."

He strides to the door. Before pulling it open, he drags in a breath and turns back to face me. His expression is unreadable, his jaw tight. "Are you going to be okay?"

"Yes." I rub my forehead. I owe him an explanation, if nothing else. "I…I have nyctophobia. It's a pathological fear of the dark that also causes my insomnia."

He frowns. "When did that start?"

"A long time ago." I avert my gaze, hating that I have to tell him about my phobias. "Therapists have told me my inability to remember the accident triggered my fear of the dark. That's why I freaked out up there. I didn't know Vanessa hadn't gotten the electricity working yet. I'll be okay if I can keep the lights on."

Something painful flashes in his eyes—an old memory, torn like regret. He gives a short nod and starts toward the door again.

"Cole."

He stops and looks at me.

"Thank you."

He grabs the door handle, his body stiffening with tension.

"Don't thank me, Josie. I never wanted you to come back to Castille. And the sooner you leave, the better."

He walks out, closing the door behind him with a hard click.

CHAPTER 3

Josie

Ten years ago

I woke in the dark. I was sitting up in the hospital bed, my head propped on a hard pillow. The curtains and the door were both closed. Only the lights of the machines gave a faint eerie glow. Shadows crawled up the walls.

My breath stuck in the middle of my chest. I fumbled for the nurse's call button and couldn't find it. Panic slithered into my veins, turning my blood to ice. I couldn't move.

The door opened with a soft click. Then his voice, a whisper barely audible over the beep of the machines.

"Josie."

Tears flooded my eyes and spilled over. A sob choked my throat. I sensed him hesitate, hovering uncertainly in the doorway. I hadn't seen him since…

He'd been taking a picture of me and my family in the foyer of
the Seagull Inn as my parents' twenty-fifth anniversary party was
winding down. I remembered the smell of wildflowers and the
flash of the camera.

Then my mind yielded nothing. An empty wasteland of
blackness. A week ago, I'd woken up in the hospital, and my sister
told me about the car accident I'd survived but couldn't remember. The one that had killed our parents and brother. In the days
since, Vanessa had barred Cole from visiting me.

Somehow I managed to lift my hand toward him. His breath
escaped in a rush before he stepped into the room and closed the
door. Then his hand closed around mine, big and warm. I turned
to face him.

"Lights," I whispered.

He turned on the lamp beside the bed. He was ashen, gray, his
face edged with hollows and black smudges of despair. Everything about him was hunched, caved in, destroyed.

"I didn't know if you'd want to see me." The words were
scratchy and rough. "I had to sneak in."

"I'm glad you did."

I hadn't known if I wanted to see him either. My wishes for
us, for our life together, had always centered on the way we were
before, the place to which we could never return. For a week,
thousands of questions about Cole had boiled among all the
others.

What new shape would our love take in this darkness? Would
I ever be able to lie beside him again, touch his warm, living skin,
and not burn with rage that Teddy's life had been cut short? That
my little brother would never know what it was like to be a man?
Would I ever be able to sit across from Cole at the dinner table
and not think of the meals he'd shared with my family? Would I
ever be able to look at his hands, at him, and not *feel* the searing,
breathtaking torture of immeasurable loss?

I didn't know. But now that he was here, holding my hand the way he'd done countless times before, the fire in my heart eased a little.

He was my steady ground, my anchor. I had no idea how I would survive this horror, but the only way through it was *with him.*

"I want you..." He stopped, his throat working with a swallow. Tears glistened in his eyes. "I want you to know how much I love you. I mean, I know you *know,* but if there's...if I could change anything, if I could—"

"Stop." My insides were scraped raw. I would never stop bleeding.

My neck ached from looking up at him. I moved over and nodded to the side of the bed. He sat, his shoulders slumping. His familiar scent beneath the antiseptic hospital air filled my senses —citrus, salt water, Cole.

In that instant, my life, my being, split in two. Before and after. I couldn't picture any kind of future. There was nothing beyond *now* except a black, empty space of despair.

Cole tightened his hand on mine. I pushed away from the pillows and edged toward him. And because he knew me so well, even in that moment, he released my hand and opened his arms.

We broke together. Harsh, painful sobs rose from us at the same time. He closed his arms tight around me, his body shaking uncontrollably. I pressed my face against the front of his shirt, gripping the cotton in my fists. We cried and cried, gasping for breath, our bodies heaving. His tears dampened my hair, ran down my cheek, my neck.

I sobbed against his chest, pressing myself impossibly close, like I needed him imprinted on my skin. We held each other as hard as we could—fingers clutching, muscles straining, both of us fighting violently against what had happened, what was inevitable.

"*God*, Josie, I'm so sorry." His voice rasped with agony. "So fucking sorry. If I could do it all differently, if I could turn the world on its axis for you, I would. I'd do anything for you. *Anything*. That will never change. No matter what happens."

I had never known such pain, like the universe was imploding inside me. Like the plates of the earth were breaking apart in my soul.

I eased away from him, wiping my wet face with the sleeve of my hospital gown. "I don't…" My breath hitched sharply. "I don't blame you, Cole. I never…I want you to know I'll never think it was your *fault*. That you did something wrong. You didn't."

His jaw clenched, and his eyes burned. "If I hadn't done something *wrong*, none of this would have happened."

"It was…" I swallowed. Though it seared my throat, I forced the word out. "…an accident."

Holy fucking God.

The endless black pit beneath me opened wider, threatening to swallow me whole.

Spilled milk was an *accident*. A stubbed toe was an *accident*. Hell, a fender-bender was a goddamned *accident*.

This? This had no words. No definition. The newspapers had called it a *tragedy*. Shakespeare wrote fucking *tragedies*.

This was absolute darkness borne of chaos, untouched by even a particle of light, a subterranean cavern where you saw nothing, heard nothing. A place where you could go insane.

"Josie." Cole gripped the sides of my head, forcing me to look at him. Every emotion crashing and burning through me was reflected in the grooves of his face, the blistered pain in his eyes.

"I love you," he said hoarsely. "So fucking much. I always will."

I curled my hands around his wrists. His pulse beat fast against my fingertips, like the heartbeat of a man on the verge of panic.

"I love you, Cole." Fresh tears rose to my reddened eyes and spilled over. "I think I fell in love with you that Halloween night when I was nine years old. Even now, I...I can't imagine loving anyone else. But how am I going to survive this?"

The question speared my already shredded heart. My body could not possibly have been made to withstand such pain.

Cole tensed, a muscle ticking violently in his jaw like he was waging an internal war. His pulse increased against my fingers. He slid his hands down to the sides of my neck, his thumb brushing the skin underneath my jaw. Suddenly, not even his gentle touch, which had always been so powerful *before*, could elicit even the tiniest pinpoint of light.

"It was my fault." The words were low, serrated, ripped from somewhere deep inside him. "And you don't have to fight another battle. I won't let you. That's why I'm leaving."

Though part of me understood the meaning of his statement, my brain couldn't process its implications.

"L-leaving?"

"Castille." He tucked a lock of my hair behind my ear, like he didn't want to stop touching me. "I'll go down to Boston, New York. Somewhere."

"But..." The horror of my irrevocably altered life took on a new dimension. A future without Cole? I had never imagined such a thing. I couldn't.

"You can't go." I grabbed his T-shirt. "I won't let you."

"I have to."

"You *have to* leave me?" Shock bolted through me, sparking a new fire of anger. "You *have* to leave me all alone after what just happened?"

He forced his gaze from me. His throat worked with a gulp. "You're not alone. Every single person in this town will do anything for you. But that's not the case with me, and if I stay, it could make things even worse for you."

"Bullshit." My anger intensified, burning in my blood. "It's your father, isn't it? Vanessa told me he's on a rampage about the *rumors*, all worried it's going to hurt his business. Is he making you do this?"

"No. It's my decision."

I didn't know if that was better or worse than thinking Kevin Danforth was forcing his son out of town. I had no answers, no clarity, no understanding. All I had was pain and the knowledge that I couldn't live if I lost Cole too.

I grabbed a tissue from the bedside tray. "You're a goddamned coward, if you think leaving me is the right thing to do."

"You'll never get through this if I stay."

"I'll never get through this if you leave."

"Josie." He slipped his hand beneath my chin and lifted my face. His eyes were bloodshot and bleak, his dark eyelashes spiky with tears. But behind his despair, tenderness gleamed.

"Promise me you'll live your life." A plea slashed his voice. "That you'll never stop creating. Promise me you'll be..." He paused and scrubbed his eyes with the back of his hand. "Promise me you'll be okay. Maybe even happy again one day. I can't live without knowing that. Please."

His tone had such a dark ring of finality that the edges of my vision splintered.

"*Happy?*" I spat the word at him. "You think I can be *happy* again?"

"I want you to be." His hand shook against my cheek. "I *need* you to be."

"Get the fuck away from me." I slapped his hand away from my face, trembling so much my teeth chattered. "You want to know what I need? I need my mother to walk in the door and hold me. I need my father to come in and tell me a bad joke. I need to hear Teddy's laugh. And if I can't have that, god*dammit*, then I need *you*. I can't survive this without you. I can't."

He didn't respond. A hard tension laced his muscles, one I'd seen before. It meant he was reinforcing himself, intensifying his strength and determination. It meant he wouldn't back down.

"Cole…"

I took hold of his T-shirt again, searching his gaze. For the first time ever, I looked into his eyes and couldn't find him there.

"You can't have me around." He unhooked my fingers from his shirt. Sudden remoteness infused him. "And I can't be with you, Josie. I can't be a constant reminder of what you lost. And every time I look at you…I'd…I'd *know* what I did. It would destroy us, everything we've ever had. I won't let that happen."

I grabbed his arm, all the rage and fury I'd screamed at the universe hardening into an arrow pointed straight at him.

"*You* are destroying everything we had!" My voice became shrill, cracked. "And how dare you make decisions about my life without me? I thought you were better than that. Instead the most horrific thing in the world happens, and you walk out on me? What the fuck kind of man are you anyway?"

His shoulders slumped, raw pain etching lines on his face. He tugged his arm from my grip.

"No!" Panic flared anew. Tears spilled down my cheeks. "Cole, please…"

"I love you." He stopped, putting his callused hand over mine. "But you can't be okay or happy again if you're with me. We both know that. It's the only reason I'm leaving."

My chest burned. "So that's it, then? You're running away?"

He didn't respond, but the tortured look in his eyes splintered my already-shattered heart into a million more pieces.

I wouldn't be able to stop him. Just like I couldn't stop the accident. Couldn't stop or change any of it.

In that instant, my love for him began to mutate, transforming into something misshapen and ugly.

"If you leave me now, I'll never forgive you." I fisted the bedcovers so hard my knuckles hurt. "I will *hate* you, Cole Danforth. I will hate you for the rest of my godforsaken life."

He hesitated. For a split-second, I saw him waver. Then he stiffened again, pulling his strength together.

"Good." He rubbed his sleeve over his face and turned to the door. "Hate me. Be mad at me. Rage. Put it all on me so you don't constantly wonder *what if*. Live your life. Please."

What fucking life?

I could hardly see him through the red mist of fury coating my vision. He was destroying the last thing I had left. My fists clenched and unclenched. Blood boiled through my skin.

He paused, his back to me. The air thickened. Then he turned and rushed toward me, closing the distance between us in less than a second. He grabbed my shoulders and hauled me against his chest.

I stiffened, resisting the urge to throw my arms around him, though I buried my face in his neck, breathed him in for what I knew, with sick, black despair, was the last time.

"I loved you before we were even born." He pressed his face to my hair. "I'd never leave you, not if I didn't have to. You will always be my best friend, and wherever you are in the world, whatever happens, please believe all I ever want is for you to be safe and happy. I'll do anything for you except stay. Anytime, anywhere, for as long as we live. *Anything*. Remember that." He detached himself from me slowly, bent to kiss my cheek, and whispered, "I love you, my Josie Bird."

The words slammed against the armor locking into place around my heart. I put my hands on his chest and shoved him away as hard as I could.

He stumbled back, his face a mask of agony. He stared at me one last time. Then he turned and walked out the door.

I collapsed against the pillow and cried until my bones ached. Pain sliced me in half. My sobs became screams of hysterical fury. Nurses ran in with sedatives. Right before the drugs pulled me under, I knew.

My love for Cole was gone, demolished by his abandonment as if obliterated by a wrecking ball. And in its place, resentment

took root and slithered black and slimy through all of our *good*.
Eating it alive.

He was gone. My best friend. The love of my life. The young
man who'd been driving the car when it veered off the road and
crashed, killing both my parents and my twelve-year-old brother.

CHAPTER 4

Cole

Present

F*uck fuck fuck.*
  I slam my bedroom door and stalk to the window, my fists clenching. My shoulders are stiff enough to break. Josie Mays is back in Castille. It's like I've been thrown into a maze of mirrors where everything is distorted and fucked up. She was never supposed to come back. I sure as hell was never supposed to see her again.

And now…she's not only here, she's already at my house.

Nyctophobia? Insomnia?

It's a knife in my gut to discover her psyche is still that tortured a decade after the crash. It shouldn't have happened that way. She was supposed to heal or, at the very least, mend.

What else has she been forced to endure? Knowing her deep scars will always bleed under the surface has been horror enough. But I'd hoped with everything in me that she'd have found something resembling peace by now.

Why the *hell* did I follow her to the cottage?

I drag a hand down my face, reliving the shadowed image of her on the cottage floor, curled into herself and shaking so hard her teeth rattled.

Before she left the pier, she was scared. I saw it in her, felt it like a live wire. All my old instincts rushed to the surface in a torrent, as if I'd never fought to bury them deep. Would she be okay, going into the cottage for the first time in over ten years?

I hadn't been able to stop myself from going after her. Just to make sure she got there okay.

And when I'd found the door open, all lights off, no sound, then her on the floor...*fucking hell*. The flashlight beam had caught her face, and she'd looked at me with a fear reserved for the devil himself.

Everything I'd told myself disappeared. The only thing left was the primal need to make sure she was safe.

That used to be my second nature. Never thought I *couldn't*.

But now the coin could flip any second. My need to protect her could end up destroying her.

I stare out the window, imagining her in the reflection on the glass. She's both the same and different. Her straight dark hair is shorter, reaching her shoulders in a thick curtain. Her features are finely etched—straight, narrow nose, high cheekbones, those thick-lashed green eyes that I couldn't look into without losing part of myself.

But she has a severity she hadn't had before, not back when she was the sweet, talented girl who smelled like cherries and was constantly forgetting something. Keys, wallet, a hairband, a goodbye kiss.

How many times did I call her from the apartment balcony as she was hurrying out the door? *"Josie, you forgot..."* whatever it was.

She'd sigh and look irritated with herself, but then we'd meet on the stairs and I'd hand over her keys or her research paper, and she'd respond with a warm kiss and a squeeze around my waist, both of which made me look forward to the next time she forgot something.

Then she'd fly out the door, her chocolate-colored ponytail streaming behind her, and I couldn't wait until the end of the day when we were home again. When we could shut the door and be alone together. The place we both loved the most.

I still taste her name in my mouth. It used to be my favorite word, even if I haven't said it aloud in years. But it's gone through my head a million times, always attached to a question. *Where is she? How is she? Is she happy?*

I can't tell if she is. Sure as hell couldn't ask. The shock of seeing her sitting in the car was like an earthquake. My heart almost beat out of my chest. And when she approached me, it was all I could do not to touch her.

Even though she was wearing jeans and an army jacket, I pictured her body. Round breasts that used to fit perfectly in my hands, curved waist that I'd grip when she was riding me, that bitable, heart-shaped ass…

Fuck.

I'm a bastard. Her first night in the town where she'd lived through hell, and I'm thinking about her naked. Just one of the many reasons I never wanted to see her again. She'll destroy my guard.

I can't let her. *Won't.*

In the distance, the downstairs shower starts. A groan breaks my chest. Now she's fully naked in my head, water streaming over her hair as she lathers soap over her breasts…

If seeing her had been a shock, touching her had been unbearable. She'd fit against me as if ten years hadn't passed. As if a No Man's Land of barbed wire and land mines didn't lie between us. A soft, warm bundle tucked right against my side.

Stop. You need to get rid of her, not have sappy thoughts about her.

Resisting the instinct not to leave her alone again, I grab the keys to my Porsche and head downstairs. I'd driven my Bentley to the wedding reception earlier tonight, and I'll have to pick it up tomorrow.

I pause at the second-floor landing. Light shines under the door of the guest bedroom where Josie is staying.

Irritation rips through me. I can't leave without telling her. What if she comes looking for me? I stop at the guest bedroom and rap my knuckles on the door.

She pulls it open. A time portal throws me back eleven years. I'm looking at my Josie Bird with her wet, tousled hair, the over-sized *Art Attack* T-shirt that hides all her soft curves, her faded Indian-print pajama pants.

Five minutes from now, we'll be tangled together on the bed, exchanging deep kisses while I edge my hand up her shirt. I can already taste her, everything sweet. Cherry lip balm. Bubble gum. Jolly Ranchers.

The urge to sweep her into my arms, lift her up against me, seizes me with crushing force. I step back, curling my hands into fists.

"I'm going out again."

A crease appears between her eyes. "Okay."

"I wanted…" I clear my throat, fighting not to stare at her breasts, her hard nipples poking against her shirt. "Wanted to let you know."

She nods. "Thank…well, have fun."

I pivot on my heel and stalk downstairs, the keys digging into my palm. The mind-numbing small talk and socializing at the wedding reception will dull my senses.

I drive my Porsche out of the gate. I'd sold my father's house, twenty miles south of here, right after he died. I bought Cliff Haven two years later—a stupid, over-the-top testament to Invicta Spirits' success and the fact that I'd crushed my father's business to dust, leaving no trace of the Iron Horse Brewery or Kevin Danforth's influence. Proving my company was now paramount.

Not that I give a shit about Castille. I'd hated the town that revered my asshole father and failed to protect my mother.

Josie had been the good part of Castille—the curious, energetic girl in the woods, the talented artist and bird lover, the tempting young woman I couldn't resist. Her close, happy family had been the opposite of mine. I'd liked her artsy mother, her father who knew a million riddles and jokes, her Lego-obsessed brother, her elegant sister.

And Josie above all, the woman who gave me the hope of a future.

Christ. A split-second happens, and suddenly you're living someone else's life.

Except that it's yours.

ॐ

I return to The Ivy, a Michelin-starred restaurant owned by an old friend of my father's. I've never liked the place with its hard-core elegance and pretentious menu. Unfortunately, I've spent more time here than my father probably did.

The main room with the picture window overlooking the water is still crowded with people dancing and eating cake. I make my way around the tables to the bride and groom. A hand closes on my arm.

"There you are." Evelyn Rockwell smiles at me. Blonde, killer body, expertly made-up face, she's as perfect now in her lacy sheath dress and heels as she was at the start of the wedding ceremony. "I thought you'd left without saying goodbye."

"I'm leaving soon."

"Where were you?"

Josie appears in my head again. Ragged army jacket and torn jeans.

Evelyn's perfume wafts into my nose, too floral and strong. I peel her hand off my arm.

"Nowhere."

Her mouth twists. "You've been gone for well over two hours. I know. I was looking for you."

"Then stop looking."

"*Cole.*" She grabs my arm again, her eyes hardening for an instant before she smiles sweetly. "Don't be mean. Give me one dance."

"No."

"Please?"

I yank my arm from her taloned grip and walk away. She and I had fucked numerous times over the past few months before I ended it when she got clingy. While I liked her naked, I'd never had intentions of getting involved with her on any other level. She knew that. They all did, right at the start. It never stopped them from coming after me, but I'd been stripped of illusions years ago.

Women wanted the fortune of Invicta Spirits, which was one of the top ten producers of distilled liquor in the country. I started the company after working for a hydropower corporation in New York, where I learned how I could leverage the control of water. My goal had been to crush my father's business and to gain power over the town that had failed both me and my mother.

The Iron Horse had been a small but popular brewery, producing a variety of craft beers. A regular crowd gathered at the pub on weekends to drink and listen to live music. My father was always in the center of it, reveling in his popularity, talking, laughing, making sure everyone was taken care of.

Before he came home and turned into the fucking devil.

I've had few greater pleasures in life than watching Kevin

Danforth sign the papers selling me the Iron Horse, whose output and profits had been sliding downhill since his diagnosis.

Say goodbye to your legacy, you old bastard.

By then, Invicta Spirits had already surpassed some of the top liquor companies on the east coast. The Iron Horse hadn't been my only target. I've pushed dozens of smaller local companies and distilleries out of business. Increased our revenue and profits tenfold. A couple more buyouts, and I'd expand even further into the south and midwest. An oil spill drowning everything in its path.

The local residents don't like it. They need the economic boost I've brought to the area, but they hate that I'm killing independent distilleries and skirting the law. Even more, they hate the fact that I control their water supply. The interesting thing is they can't do anything about it.

I start toward the bride and groom again. My uncle is standing near the bar. Before I can divert around him, he catches my eye and indicates his companion—an attractive, sharp-eyed woman in her mid-fifties wearing a beaded dress.

I bite back a groan. Allegra King and I have locked horns countless times over city ordinances and zoning laws, not to mention my purchase of the Spring Hills water well. Now she's partly responsible for Josie returning to Castille.

Uncle Gerald waves me over, his expression pointed. My mother's older brother, he lived in New York for most of my childhood, then moved to Castille after joining Invicta Spirits. I hadn't seen much of him when I was younger, but we'd reconnected when I moved to New York after the accident. He'd always been a straight shooter, a man I've felt I could trust.

Steeling my spine, I approach him and Allegra. "Hello, Allegra. You look lovely."

She nods with disdain, but her tone is polite. "Thank you, Cole."

"I just ran into Josie Mays."

Her eyes widen. Gerald turns to stare at me.

"Josie *Mays?*" he repeats, as if there's some other Josie I might be talking about.

"We weren't expecting her until next week," Allegra says.

"We?" I clench my teeth.

She composes herself, lifting an eyebrow. "Much as you might believe otherwise, Colton, you're not the only person of influence in this town. When Josie told me the proposal to honor her parents had been abandoned so many years ago due to lack of financing, I knew I had to support her. Benjamin and Faith Mays were vibrant, active members of this community, and they deserve to be remembered well. Having their daughter paint a mural of Castille's history is the way we intend to honor them. If you have a problem with that, you take it up with me. Not her."

"Damn straight I have a problem with that." I make an effort to keep my voice low. "Where is this mural going to be?"

"Lantern Square." She sips her drink, her tone deceptively casual. "On the wall of the Botanical Gardens."

My chest tightens. The perimeter of the Botanical Gardens is primarily surrounded by a wrought-iron fence, but one section is composed of an old masonry wall that had been built about the same time as the garden construction. That is the only area where a mural can be painted.

It's also fifty feet from my office. *On my property*, a fact that Allegra clearly doesn't know.

I won't tell her. Yet. I haven't gotten to where I am by showing my hand too early.

"Where is the money coming from to fund the mural?" I ask.

"We diverted funds from the Arts Center construction since this will be a public art project. We plan to unveil the mural at the Bicentennial Festival in August."

"The festival Invicta Spirits is sponsoring?"

"Not that the mural will affect our sponsorship." Gerald gives me a warning glare. "Allegra, I'm sure you understand Cole's objections, given everything that happened. But he won't cause any trouble."

That's what you think.

"I would hope not." Though her tone is light, suspicion glints in Allegra's expression. "In fact, your uncle and I were just discussing how Invicta Spirits can become further involved in the festival. We'd like you to attend our next committee meeting."

I expel a hard breath. Fucking festival.

"I'm sure my uncle will be pleased to take my place at the meeting," I reply. "He has full autonomy regarding our company's role and sponsorship."

She smiles tightly. "We'd be remiss if we didn't include you, Cole. As the company owner and CEO, it's rather important that we have your input. Friday afternoon at two, City Hall. We'll look forward to seeing you there."

She gives us both a swift nod of farewell and strides away.

"Cole, you have got to play the goddamned game," Gerald snaps, his voice low. "Castille is this close to taking Invicta to court over the water pump station you're building at Spring Hills. The company lawyers are sweating bullets. If you don't get onboard, you'll be dealing with a class-action lawsuit instead of a stupid pie-eating contest."

I don't care. I'd *welcome* a fucking lawsuit. Then I could spend every waking hour fighting it. Filling my brain with strategies and plans instead of obsessing over the woman who will be living in Watercolor Cottage for the next two months.

I need to get rid of her.

"I'll be at the meeting," I tell Gerald.

Relief flashes over his face. I start to turn away. He grabs my arm.

"And you *cannot* be talking shit about Josie Mays," he says pointedly. "You will always take the heat for what happened, but that girl is untouchable. Her family was well-loved around here. If you act like you don't care about her, and I *know* that's a fucking lie even if no one else does, the residents of this town will forget a damned lawsuit and run you out of here with torches and pitchforks."

Yanking my arm away from him, I take a step back.

"Cole, how is she?" Gerald's voice has a sudden note of gentleness.

My back teeth clench. How *is* she? She's as brave as a warrior and as soft as a bluebird. She's all the good parts of my life here—warm sand, fresh-cut grass, oranges, peppermint sticks. She's fiery green eyes and skin like cream. She's a wild, broken paint stroke.

"Alive." The word snaps out of me like a whip.

Turning away from my uncle, I stride toward the front door.

I should fire him. He's my guilty conscience. If I get rid of him, there'd be nothing preventing me from doing whatever the hell I want with the company. There'd be no one forcing me to sponsor a small-town festival that I couldn't give a shit about. No one who really knows how I used to feel about Josie.

"Cole."

I turn to face Allegra, who is putting on her shawl. She gestures me closer.

"You listen to me," she says, her tone sharp. "I know this is hard for you, but I will not have you making things difficult for that girl."

"You mean the girl who's going to be painting a goddamned mural fifty feet from my office?" I lift an eyebrow. "I'm surprised at you, Allegra. I thought you were the kind of woman who'd say *fuck you* to my face instead of engaging in passive-aggressive bullshit."

Irritation hardens her features. "We did not plan this as retaliation. The city council chose the garden wall as the mural site because it's in the center of town and will have the most visibility. Also that wall has been an eyesore for years. The mural will give the entire square a much-needed beautification. Besides…"

She tosses her shawl over her shoulder and shrugs. "If you don't like the mural, you can always move your office out of Lantern Square."

Despite my anger, I experience a grudging respect toward her. She's always proven to be a worthy adversary, and I love a good fight. She's been wanting me—and the reminder of Invicta Spirits—out of Lantern Square for years. And under any other circumstances, I'd enjoy going head-to-head with Allegra King.

But this time, Josie is in the middle.

Hell. Josie *started* it.

"I'm not going anywhere," I tell Allegra flatly.

"Then if you don't want to make an enemy out of everyone in this town, you need to start working with us instead of against us. I understand it's difficult for you to have Josie Mays back in Castille, but—"

"I'm sorry, Allegra." I back away from her. "But you don't understand a fucking thing."

I stalk back out to my car and place a call to my assistant.

"Find out everything you can about Castille's public art ordinances. I want every single detail on my desk by tomorrow morning."

I end the call and toss the phone onto the passenger seat. My blood is hot. I should go somewhere else—a bar, a club. Call an old girlfriend for a fuck.

Instead I return home and park beside Josie's rental car in the driveway. A light still burns in the guest bedroom.

Does she sleep at all? Or is she so scared of the dark that she can't even close her eyes? What is that doing to her?

I toss my keys on the entryway table and stride upstairs. Though I have every intention of climbing the next set of stairs to the third floor, I turn toward Josie's room again.

The door is partway open. A triangle of light shines on the hallway carpet. Tension grips my neck. Placing my hand flat on the door, I ease it fully open. All the lights are on.

My heartbeat kicks into gear. She's sprawled on her stomach in the middle of the bed, her arms and legs outstretched like a starfish, her face buried in a pillow and her dark hair spilling over her shoulders. Her body moves with quick shallow breaths, not like the heavy rhythm I remember when she'd snuggle up against my side and sleep until ten a.m.

She twitches. A faint moan escapes her throat. I almost start forward...to do what, I don't know. Touch her? Comfort her? I want to do both. I curl my fingers into my palms.

She turns her head on the pillow. Her hair flops to the other side. Her eyes are closed, her skin flushed.

I track my gaze over her body. Her cotton pajama pants hug her perfect dumpling ass, and her T-shirt is pulled up enough to expose the smooth bare skin of her lower back.

Goddamn.

I'm a fucking pervert creeping in on her like this, but I can't stop staring at her. The warm hollow where her spine curves was my favorite place on her. I'd loved rubbing her back and pressing kisses along the ridge of her spine. In public, I'd put my hand on her lower back to remind both her and any other guy who might be watching that she was mine.

That smooth expanse of skin was *one* favorite out of a thousand. There was no part of Josie that wasn't my favorite. Every time I touched her, it felt like I was discovering something new.

She shifts again, rubbing her cheek on the pillow. Lust fills my chest. I feel her, slick and hot. I hear her moans, that little gasping *"Oh, Cole"* that always caught in the back of her throat.

Everything—her soft flesh yielding to my grip, her back arching. She was a firecracker—a slow, hot burn; a sharp explosion, a wild sparkler.

She was mine.

Josie opens her eyes. Our gazes collide. A charge fires between us, swift and potent.

"What are you doing here?" Her sleep-thick voice, serrated at the edges, pours into my veins and vibrates against my skin. I'd give anything to hear her whisper my name in that voice again.

"Nothing." I step toward the door. "Just got back."

She pushes to one elbow and shoves her hair away from her face. Her gaze slides over me and stops on the heaviness in my trousers. She blinks, like she's not sure what she's seeing.

Then a pink flush rises to her cheeks, and her lips part so temptingly it's all I can do not to grab her and haul her against me. Crush her mouth with mine. Eat her up.

Guilt slices through me. I turn to the door. "Go back to sleep, Josie."

As if it's easy for her.

I leave, shutting the door behind me. My breath burns my chest. I stride back to my room and yank open the balcony doors. The sea air washes over my hot skin. I lean my arms on the railing and lower my head.

My lust for her, even more powerful after ten years apart, is just *one* reason I can't have her in town. There are a thousand more.

I can't stand the thought of her being confronted by reminders of the accident. What if she hears the rumors again or discovers all the shit that went down after she left? What will that do to her? She'll be caught in a fucking avalanche of new phobias, maybe worse than what she already has.

I won't let that happen. I failed her once. I won't do it again. This time, I *will* protect her.

And the only way to protect her is to force her to leave. If that means making her hate me, good. I'll take the hit.

It won't be easy. But if I don't, my worst nightmare could come true.

CHAPTER 5

Josie

I stare at the bedroom ceiling. For once, I can't blame *this* wide-awake state on insomnia or night terrors. Blood rushes thickly through my veins, and a throb pulses low in my belly. For the hundredth time, I tell myself I was imagining the hard bulge in Cole's trousers.

As he stood watching me while I slept. Which should totally creep me out. Except it doesn't. Because despite everything, it's still Cole.

With a groan, I press my hands to my eyes. Not even the catastrophic end of our relationship had weakened my body's need for him. I'd gone without sex for two years after the accident before finally giving in to a nice young sculptor I'd been tentatively dating. He'd been caring and attentive, but I hadn't *felt* anything near what I'd experienced with Cole. And though my relationship with the sculptor lasted for another three months, it was never free from Cole's shadow.

Nothing was. Especially not my heart.

I rub my hand restlessly over my breasts. Despite my shock at waking from a shallow sleep and finding him hovering over me, my body had responded to him with lightning-quick speed.

I trail my fingers along the waistband of my pants. Strongly tempted as I am to reach into them and touch myself, I resist the urge. Over the past decade, I've often fantasized about all the dirty things Cole and I had done—which I still *wanted*.

But I've also had plenty of fantasies about gentler moments— slow, deep kisses, his long fingers trailing between my breasts, me nuzzling my face into the curve of his shoulder that smelled like sun and salt. All of those images always featured Cole and me as we were *before*.

A deep ache of longing rises in me. In our blissful college days, we'd had a wild, wonderful sex life, full of youthful enthusiasm. I'd wanted to experience everything with him. He'd been as eager and impassioned as I was—even more so—and we'd indulged in each other whenever we had the chance.

Our lovemaking had contained everything from slow, romantic interludes to hard quickies in questionable places. A secluded area of the woods, the backseat of the car while parked near the lighthouse, the kitchen table. Aside from the excitement and intense pleasure, we'd had a lot of outright fun.

We'd also been in love.

But now? He's not the fervent young man whose hands trembled when he touched my naked body. He's not adventurous or playful or impatient.

He's hard. In more ways than one. *Intense*. And aside from the fact that he clearly doesn't want me here, I'm in no position to contend with a man like him, even in my fantasies. No matter what my body says to the contrary.

I pull my hand reluctantly from under my shirt. Unfulfilled need courses through me. Knowing sleep will be more elusive than ever, I sit up and grab my sketchbook from the nightstand, hoping to distract myself with drawings.

When dawn breaks, I listen tautly for any sound of Cole, but the house is silent. I take a quick shower, gather my things, and walk cautiously down the winding staircase. A glance out the front window tells me Cole's Porsche is gone.

Disbelief clouds my mind again. I'm not surprised he's so successful, but the path he took is never one I would have imagined for him.

Then again, my phobia-riddled life isn't one I would have imagined for me.

I find my car keys on the entryway table and head outside, breathing in the welcome sea air.

Regardless of this rather shocking encounter with Cole, it's time to focus on what I came here to do—design and paint the mural and be here for Vanessa during the last two months of her pregnancy. My reasons for returning to Castille are *good*, centering on renewal and hope.

After putting my luggage back in the trunk, I check the map on my phone to find a way to downtown Castille that doesn't involve Highway 16 along the coastline or the Old Mill Bridge that crosses an ocean inlet.

A text appears from Vanessa that she's leaving Portland early and will text me when she's back. *Come to the house for tea.*

Pleased at the invitation, I drive to downtown Castille. Living in San Francisco, I haven't had to battle my fear of driving too often, but as long as it's daylight and I drive slowly, my heart rate stays reasonably calm.

After returning the car at a downtown rental office, I pop a cherry Lifesaver into my mouth and walk. Lantern Street is populated by shops, restaurants, and art galleries. Several of my old haunts—a dime store and a diner where we used to hang out after school—have closed, but overall the town hasn't changed much in ten years.

I stop and make sketches at the Castille Museum and court-house. I've already completed the mural design, but I need to study historical blueprints and city maps to make sure I'm getting everything right. I head to the archives department at Ford's College.

Situated in the library basement, the archives are accessible via a set of concrete steps and a narrow corridor lit by a single fluorescent light. The door marked *Rare Books and Archives* is locked, and I press the buzzer on the wall.

A slender, pale young woman with dark brown hair opens the door. "Miss Mays? The security guard called down to let me know you were on the way. I'm Charlotte, the librarian."

"Josie. Thanks for your time." I follow her into a large carpeted space lined with wooden tables and locked cabinets. A neatly ordered desk sits at the front of the room and three doors lead to what I assume are the stacks.

"I heard about your mural project." Charlotte runs her hands over her gray skirt. "You'd like to look at some of our architectural blueprints?"

"Yes, for the historic buildings in town. Just so I can make sure I'm getting the details right."

"If you want to sit down, I'll see what I can find." She disappears toward a door marked *Archives.*

I take out my sketchpad and pencils and sit down at a table. Another door labeled *Medieval Manuscripts* opens. A tall, strikingly handsome man dressed in a beautiful tailored navy suit and striped tie emerges, carrying two very old-looking books.

As he walks to a table, I can't help gazing at him like a fangirl staring in awe at a gorgeous movie star. He catches my eye. His smile of greeting brings a flush to my face.

Wow. Who knew the basement archives of a library could attract a man like *him*?

"See if these will do, for a start." Charlotte sets several ledgers and a large roll of papers in front of me. "These are the blueprints for the Castille Lighthouse and the Hancock House, and architectural drawings for the National Bank."

I turn my attention away from the handsome scholar and toward the papers. Charlotte reaches in front of me to turn on the desk light. Her fingernails are bitten to the quick, the skin almost raw around the edges. A habit I'm familiar with.

"I'll get you a pair of gloves." She walks to her desk, pausing to speak briefly with the scholar. I catch her calling him "Professor West." Lucky students.

After putting on the gloves, I get to work copying details of the architecture. Charlotte proves to be efficient and helpful, bringing me everything from surveys to photographs, measured drawings, and renovation records.

"Have you started the mural yet?" she asks.

"No, but I've completed the design." I show her a few rough sketches. "If I can get the wall prepped within the next couple of days, I hope to start painting next week."

"And you have all the permits and such?"

"Yes, I believe so. I'm verifying it all with Allegra King and the festival committee on Friday."

Charlotte nods. For whatever reason, she appears worried, though maybe that's just her nature. She reminds me of a little gray mouse, quiet and slightly skittish. Rather appropriate for a librarian in the isolated basement archives.

I fill several pages of my sketchbook with drawings before my stomach reminds me I haven't eaten breakfast yet. Stacking the archival records on the table, I approach the desk where Charlotte and Professor West are conversing.

"Thanks again, Charlotte," he says. "I'll be back soon to look at the psalters." He steps aside as if he's making room for me, giving us both a polite nod of farewell. "Enjoy the rest of your day, ladies."

Picking up a leather briefcase, he walks out of the library. A brief silence follows in his wake before I realize both Charlotte and I are watching him go.

"He's just visiting." She smiles ruefully at me. "He makes occasional trips out here to study our medieval manuscript collection."

"Oh. He's...impressive."

"Yes. He's also extremely married."

I blink and stammer, "I didn't mean...I wasn't..."

"Don't worry about it." She waves a hand and turns to the computer. "His wife is lovely too. He's just one of those men who has...*something*."

Like Cole. Who once had *something* that was far more appealing and approachable to me. Something I'd loved.

"Let me get you a card." Charlotte types on the keyboard. "We can keep a record of your materials."

She scans a library card for me and inputs my information into the computer.

"Is that Persian?" I nod toward an intricate silver amulet dangling from her desk lamp.

"Turkish." She takes the amulet and hands it to me. "It's called a *nazar*, a charm against the evil eye."

"It's beautiful." I rub my finger over the smooth blue-and-white stone in the center. "My mother once incorporated evil-eye protection into several paintings of sacred geometry mandalas."

"I've seen some of her work at the museum. She was so talented."

Bittersweet sorrow fills me. I've often wondered what other creative avenues my mother would have taken, had she lived.

A fleeting consternation rises to Charlotte's eyes. "I'm sorry, I didn't mean to—"

"No, it's all right. I love knowing that her work is still appreciated." I extend the amulet.

"Keep it," she says.

"Oh, I can't..."

"No, really." She pushes the amulet back toward me. "I'd like you to have it. For good luck and protection."

Heaven knows I could use both.

"Thank you." Warmed by the kind gesture, I slip the amulet into my pocket. "That's really nice of you."

"I hope it works." She hands me the library card and turns back to her computer.

After thanking her again, I head upstairs and back out into the sunshine.

As I walk toward Lantern Street, I spot the towers of the Seagull Inn, a huge converted Victorian house with towers jutting up at the corners.

My blood ices over and my breath shortens. I turn in the opposite direction. One day I'll have to face it, maybe even go inside, but that won't be anytime soon.

No. Stopping in my tracks, I force myself to return to the restaurant. I will not allow fear to rule me any longer.

Touching the evil-eye amulet in my pocket, I make it to the front porch before my legs weaken. I can almost hear the music, the laughter, the lively conversation of my parents' anniversary party. I walk up the stairs and enter.

"Table for one?" the hostess asks me.

"No, I...I'm not here to eat, thanks."

Though she furrows her brow, she nods and returns to the dining room. I let my gaze roam over the spot where I'd stood with my parents, the vast room where we'd celebrated.

I see the flash go off on Teddy's new camera. I see my parents —my father's hand on my mother's cheek, their love and devotion so tangible. I see Cole, his smile warm as he leans down to press his lips against mine...

The image splinters. A screeching noise, high-pitched and jarring, hits my ears. I stumble backward. My heart crashes against my ribs. I manage to turn and hurry back outside, dragging in a breath.

"Dude, be careful!" a male voice yells.

Across the street, a pedestrian flips off a driver who has skidded to a halt at the crosswalk. Several people stop to watch the altercation. The two men exchange a few insults. The driver revs the engine and peels away.

I press a hand to my pounding heart.

"He wasn't going to stop for a pedestrian in the *crosswalk*." A woman standing in front of the restaurant catches my eye and shakes her head with disapproval.

Since she appears to expect a response, I say, "That's terrible."

"You have to be so careful these days." She tugs the leash of a tiny dog and starts walking. "People drive like maniacs. Good thing he didn't kill someone."

Sharp pain knots in my chest. I descend the porch steps and hurry away.

❧

As I continue walking, the morning sun and salty air ease my dismay. I stop at the library, the bakery where I had my first job, the art gallery that sold my very first painting when I was nineteen years old. To my pleasure, the people whom I'd known before the accident greet me with delight.

"Josie, how wonderful to see you again. We were so happy to hear you were coming back."

"I knew you'd be a successful artist! I love that you'll be painting a mural for the town."

"Welcome home, Josie. You didn't think I'd forget your favorite, did you? Chocolate croissant on the house."

After last night's breakdown and the shock of seeing Cole again, it's a decided relief to rediscover the warmth of my hometown.

I walk to Lantern Square, the central part of town and site of summer concerts and the farmer's market. The nineteenth-century courthouse and bell tower preside over a large, tree-dotted lawn, with colorful shops, restaurants, and coffee-houses arranged around a brick-paved pedestrian plaza. It's the oldest part of town, the architecture characterized by gingerbread trim, gables, and rounded archways.

The only aesthetic flaw is the cracked masonry wall concealing part of the Botanical Gardens. That's where Allegra King told me I could paint the mural.

I get a takeout coffee and sit at a table in the plaza, opening my sketchbook. I draw the shops across the street, enjoying the feel of my pencil skimming over the page even if the architecture doesn't create a full-fledged burst of inspiration.

I stopped doing my whimsical animal paintings after the crash. It had taken me months to pick up a paintbrush again, and ever since my art has gone from dark, angular abstracts to black holes to the nightmarish, dystopian landscapes and disembodied heads that collectors and gallery owners admire so much.

While I'm grateful my work has caught people's attention, and that they pay me for it, I'm increasingly uncomfortable selling art borne of tragedy and pain. Isn't there enough of that in the world?

"Josie?"

I glance up at a police cruiser parked at the curb. A handsome blond officer closes the driver's side door and crosses the side-walk. Pleasure rises in me. Nathan Peterson and his family had lived in Castille for as long as ours had, and he'd been one grade ahead of me throughout school.

I smile. "Hi, Nathan."

"I thought that was you." He steps forward, one arm tentatively outstretched. "I've heard all about your return and your mural project. It's great to see you again."

I rise and return his embrace. After graduation, he'd gone to the Maine Criminal Justice Academy and had been a rookie police officer the night of the accident.

"When did you get in?" he asks.

"Just last night." I step back and gesture to the lieutenant insignia on his uniform. "Look at you. You've moved up in the world."

"In Castille, at least." His eyes darken a touch. "How have you been?"

"Good. I'm happy to be back." I squeeze his hands in reassurance. If there's anything I'm not going to do, it's rehash just how bad things had gotten before I'd managed to pull myself from the despondency of loss. My wounds will never heal, but I've accepted that they'll always be part of me. It's the dark, ugly things that grew out of the pain I still need to eradicate.

"Sit down." I indicate a chair at the table. "Are you still living in town?"

"Yeah, I got a little house over at the cove." Pride rises to his eyes. "Has a boat dock and everything. I spend my weekdays working and my weekends fishing and boating, so I can't complain. I stopped by to see Vanessa when she moved back but haven't heard from her since then. She's all right?"

"She's coming in from Portland this afternoon, so I actually haven't seen her yet. But she's doing well. And your parents and brother?"

"Dad passed away a few years ago, but Mom's still living over on Hartford Street." He twists his mouth. "Richard moved out to Benton after losing his company."

My stomach tightens with remembered unpleasantness at the mention of Richard Peterson. I'd always liked Nathan, but his older brother had been a different story—a good-looking popular boy who'd used his entitled status to bully other kids.

When I was nine, Richard had tried to steal my Halloween candy, and then when I was nineteen, he'd made unwanted advances. Both times Cole had stepped in to help me.

"You're like my hero."

A humorless laugh broke from Cole's chest. "I'm no hero."

"You are to me."

I shake away the memory and focus on Nathan again. "What kind of company did your brother own?"

"He and a friend started a little bottled water company over near Fernsdown." Nathan shakes his head. "Blue River Water. They produced a natural alkaline water that was a great source of minerals. The company employed about eighty people, but they took a hit when the economy started going downhill. The owner of Invicta Spirits was the only one who offered them a loan."

My heart jumps. "Cole Danforth?"

"Yeah." Bitterness infuses his voice. "Rich should have known better."

"Why?"

"At first the loan helped Blue River get back on its feet, but Rich couldn't pay it back on the terms Danforth set. High interest, tight deadlines. Danforth refused to negotiate. Blue River went under, and my brother had to file for bankruptcy. Danforth took over the aquifer that was the source of their water. Eighty people out of work. He didn't do a fucking thing except sit on his goddamned throne and laugh."

Dismayed shock ricochets through me. Richard had been an ass, but surely Cole wasn't so vindictive as to destroy his business out of revenge?

"Why would Cole do that?"

"Because he's nothing like his father," Nathan replies. "When Danforth brought Invicta up here from New York, he outbid Castille for control of the Spring Hills water well. The *town's* main water supply. Then after he closed his father's brewery, he targeted a bunch of small distilleries and factories. Shut them down one by one. Apparently he runs his company with an iron fist too. Everyone's afraid of him."

Tension locks my shoulders. I'm afraid of him too, but for

totally different reasons. Last night proved my feelings toward him are still right at the surface of my skin. Anger, pain, bitter-sweet longing, even the fragile threads of a trust I'd thought was irrevocably broken.

Nathan rubs a hand over the back of his neck, his mouth turning downward. "Now Danforth wants to put some sort of water booster station at the spring because he's expanding into the bottled water industry. That's why he shut down Blue River. Residents are ticked off that he wants to profit from a natural resource that belongs to them. There's talk about a class-action lawsuit against Invicta."

Good lord.

I tighten my grip on my cup. I can't believe it. Cole was supposed to work in ocean conservation, studying whale and shark distribution, spearheading beach cleanups and researching marine wildlife.

Instead he's a hardcore corporate overlord crushing smaller businesses, putting people out of work, and turning the town against him? Never once would I have pictured that of him. Not the bright, ocean-loving boy with the sun-streaked hair and eyes the color of the sea.

Nathan points his chin toward the historic Snapdragon Inn, which presides with stately elegance over the southern corner of the square.

"Danforth bought the inn when the city council was consid-ering getting rid of it because it was straining the budget," he says. "Everyone hoped he'd donate the inn to the Historical Soci-ety. Instead he set up his office there."

"He moved the Invicta Spirits offices into the inn?"

"*His* office," Nathan clarifies. "The main headquarters are in the industrial park over near Benton, and the distilleries are in factories. For whatever reason, Danforth decided the company's owner and president needed a whole damned inn as his office. Probably as a big fuck you to the town. It's like a *lair*. I've heard his employees aren't allowed in without an appointment. No one is."

I frown. The Snapdragon Inn is on the other side of the masonry wall edging the Botanical Gardens. Extending halfway down the block, the wall conceals only a corner of the garden. At some point, the rest of the garden was enclosed by a wrought-iron fence that's much more aesthetically pleasing than the old wall.

Before I can process the idea of painting the mural so close to Cole's office, my phone buzzes with a text from him. *Work at the cottage is done.*

"People are pissed." Nathan pulls his eyebrows together. "The problem is that Invicta Spirits provides a lot of revenue, so there's not much anyone can do. Word is he's trying to deflect the growing protest by sponsoring the Bicentennial Festival...or his PR people are making him do it...but it'll take a lot more than that."

"I'm sorry to hear that." Even with the knowledge that Cole doesn't want me here, even with the still-festering ache over the way he'd walked out on me, I can't wrap my brain around it.

"It's all kind of shitty, but hopefully good will prevail." Nathan lifts a hand to a passerby who gives him a wave of greeting. "I don't know if the lawsuit is going forward, but I guarantee Danforth won't get away with his tactics for much longer."

I don't know what to make of any of this. I tuck my phone away and gather my things. "Nathan, it was great seeing you again."

"You too, Josie." He rises to his feet and takes my paper cup and plate to the recycling bin. "I'd like to see Vanessa again sometime as well."

He turns back to me. Though he's in the shade, a shaft of sunlight illuminates his brown eyes.

A sudden image appears in my mind, shockingly clear—

Nathan's eyes, burning red, his face pale and drawn in a dizzying kaleidoscope of darkness and flashing lights.

My heart hammers. I grab the back of the chair.

What the fuck was that?

"...staying with her?"

His voice breaks through my haze. I deflect the stabbing fear that my nightmares are starting to invade my waking hours. It's bad enough that they destroy my sleep, but if I see them during the day...?

I pull in a breath. "Sorry, what?"

"Are you staying with Vanessa?" he repeats.

"No, up at my mother's cottage near the harbor." Struggling to regain my composure, I loop my backpack over one shoulder. "I'm heading over there now. Haven't had a chance to get settled yet."

"I'll come with you, if you need a hand." He glances at his watch. "My shift is about over."

"No, that's okay." I dig into my bag for the cottage keys. "But thank you."

After saying goodbye, I hurry toward the path leading to the cove. My return to Castille is supposed to inspire hope and light. But what if I fall even deeper into the dark?

CHAPTER 6

Josie

This time, stepping into Watercolor Cottage is a pleasure. Afternoon light illuminates the old wood trim and cream-colored plaster walls. A tiled sunroom lined with windows overlooks a spectacular view of the boat-dotted cove, and a queen-sized bed rests against the wall. Wooden shelves hold glazed clay pots and an art-supply box stained with paint.

Mom.

My anxiety and confusion drain away. I set down my backpack and drink in the air as if it's the potion I've been needing. The elixir that will help heal me, inspire me, turn me into the woman I want to be.

As long as I have enough lights. Aside from the ceiling fixtures, which are dim, there's only one floor lamp. I bought an industrial-strength flashlight from a hardware store this morning, so I should be okay tonight, but I'll buy more lamps tomorrow.

After unpacking a few things, I head to the old Colonial house on Poppy Lane. Ours had always been the "artsy" house on the block with my mother's sculptures decorating the front lawn, and Teddy's toys scattered everywhere.

Now the whole lot looks shabby and worn. Patches of brown dot the lawn, the paint is flaking, and weeds poke out of the flowerbeds where my father used to plant petunias and marigolds.

I walk to the front porch, catching sight of a fat, ceramic frog nestled among the weeds. With a wide grin and a vaguely cross-eyed stare, Bartles has guarded the yard since I was five years old.

I remember the day my mother had brought the frog home from her studio, remarking that she'd made a mistake with the eyes, but she couldn't bear to part with it. My father had promptly christened the frog Bartles and placed it right beside the front walkway. Despite the fact that Bartles is no longer surrounded by colorful annuals, at least he's still in his place of honor.

The front door opens before I reach the steps. My sister comes onto the porch, her sleeveless top displaying her tanned arms, her hair falling in honey-colored waves to her shoulders. In loose black pants and an embroidered maternity top, she's a vision of willowy beauty.

"Sorry I missed your text." She holds the rickety screen door open. "I'd have been here if I'd known you were coming early."

"It's okay. The person subletting my apartment asked to move in a couple of days in advance, so I left sooner than I'd expected to."

She glances toward the driveway. "Where's your car?"

"I just got a rental at the train station." I climb the porch steps. "I returned it this morning since I can walk everywhere."

"How was the trip?"

"Fine." I stop beside her, hating the tension vibrating between us.

We look at each other, as if trying to figure out if either of us has changed. She's still lovely and elegant with her golden hair and graceful figure. I'm still...Josie in the middle. Ordinary height, brown hair, average weight.

As a nerdy artist, I'd never minded us being so different physically, but I had envied Vanessa's self-assurance and ease with people. She'd been popular and friendly, on the student council, involved with many clubs.

I'd been the odd girl who usually had her nose in a sketchbook and liked hanging out in the woods. But my sister's glow always brightened my own aura, and we'd once had a close relationship dominated by amused affection over our differences.

We reach for each other at the same time. Our embrace is awkward, due to both time and the baby bump swelling under her shirt. Briefly, I touch her belly.

No matter how hard and unpleasant things have gotten for me and my sister, she's going to have a baby. My nephew. A new person in our small, broken family. If there was ever a time to repair our strained relationship, that time is now.

I follow her into the house, bracing myself for a wave of grief that never comes. There's nostalgia, yes, and the ever-present bittersweetness of happy memories mixed with loss, but I'm more surprised than sad.

Though some things are the same—the shabby birch and maple furniture, the throw rugs covering sections of the scarred hardwood floors—so much is *gone*. Our father's books, our mother's paintings and sculptures, the shelves of knickknacks and projects Teddy had brought home from school.

"What did you do with everything?" I wave a hand to the living room.

"What do you mean?"

"Mom's art and stuff. Dad's history books."

"Oh, it's all in the basement." Vanessa heads for the kitchen. "Come on in. I just have to pour the tea."

"Do you mind if I check out the basement later?"

"Go ahead." She takes a kettle from the stove and pours water into a teapot. "If you want to take any of it with you when you leave, please do. I don't need all that stuff around."

My stomach curdling with both irritation and guilt, I sit at the table. I hadn't been here when Vanessa was finalizing the details of our parents' estate. I'd been too devastated to want to return.

She'd sent me my share of the inheritance and told me we co-owned the house, Watercolor Cottage, and a little cabin on Eagle Mountain called Heavenly Daze that had been our father's favorite place. But even three properties hadn't been enough for Vanessa.

She'd also gone after Cole for blood money. A month after the car accident, she'd filed a multi-million dollar wrongful death lawsuit against him. She'd accused him of having been driving while distracted, overtired or even possibly intoxicated.

I'd learned about the lawsuit a month before I was planning to move to San Francisco. While I'd welcomed the idea of escaping, my sister's legal action had wrought fresh anger and pain. I'd been furious with Vanessa—not because I cared about Cole any longer, but because I hadn't wanted anything from him. Certainly not his money.

"You did what?" I couldn't believe what I was hearing.

Vanessa folded her arms, her features stiff. She'd aged fifteen years in the past month. So had I. Every second of torment and loss was burned into our bones, our skin. But after our initial outpouring of grief, a strained distance had spread between us.

"He owes us," Vanessa said. "If it hadn't been for his reckless driving, they'd still be alive."

"He's not a reckless driver!" I retorted. "He never has been. It was an accident."

"An accident that wouldn't have happened if he'd been paying attention."

"He was."

"You don't know that. You can't remember. He might have been drunk, for all we know."

"He didn't have anything to drink at the party. I was there."

"So was I."

"You didn't see him drink anything." I started to shake with anger. *"No one did. And his blood test was negative."*

She rolled her eyes. *"Those tests aren't reliable."*

"Vanessa, it was raining. The car slid on that sharp curve just after Old Mill Bridge. He lost control."

"Right. He lost control. It was his fault."

"It was an accident!"

"He fucked up and killed our parents and brother!" Her voice rose to a yell. *"If he's not going to prison for that, I'll make him pay another way."*

We fought. She hired a lawyer. I'd moved to California earlier than I'd intended, refusing to have anything to do with the proceedings. I hadn't even wanted to talk to my sister for fear that she'd bring up the lawsuit.

Then less than three weeks after she'd filed the suit, she sent me an email telling me they'd reached a settlement. Cole had given her the full sum of what she'd demanded. The suit was dropped.

I'd wanted none of the money, sick at the thought that Cole had very likely been forced to either use his trust fund or ask his father for it.

Now, however, I don't want to bring up the acrimony that tore my sister and I apart. I just hope my being here is enough to convince her I want to make amends.

"Maybe we can donate some of Mom and Dad's stuff." I accept a cup of tea from her. "The museum at Ford's would love Mom's art, and we can give Dad's books to the Historical Society."

"Sure." She sits across from me with her own cup. "Get rid of whatever you want to. It doesn't matter to me."

What does? I bite back the question because the answer is

obvious. Her baby. That's what we both need to focus on. Vanessa won't want to sort through old, dusty memories, but she will want to get ready for her son.

She'd once been a talented interior designer, but her husband had wanted her to stop working after they got married. Too late, she'd discovered he'd purposely isolated her as a means of getting his hands on almost all the financial assets she'd brought to the marriage. Including the money she'd gotten from Cole.

"So you've got the mural all organized?" She pours milk into her tea.

"I'm going to a meeting about it tomorrow. Allegra King wants to have the unveiling ceremony at the Bicentennial Festival in August."

"What does that involve?"

"A ribbon-cutting ceremony, music, food. It's scheduled for the morning right before the parade."

Vanessa frowns, bringing the cup to her lips. "I don't want to attend something like that."

"Why not?"

She sighs. "Look, I'm glad you're painting the mural. I want Mom and Dad to be honored and remembered in a good way, and I know you need to do this for them. But this also means that everyone's going to be talking about it again, what a tragedy, all that crap. And then, *poor pathetic Vanessa, did you hear her husband stole her money and ran out on her? And she's pregnant on top of it all. Such a shame, she used to be so bright, homecoming queen, track star and all, and look at her now.*"

I have no response to that because it's probably the truth.

"At least you're able to come back as a success," she continues.

"God, Vanessa." I lean closer, reaching out to touch her arm. "Do you know why I've been a successful artist? Because every painting that comes out of me is a mess of pain and sharp angles. Critics call it edgy and dramatic. Young collectors love it. And yes, I've found a catharsis in what I do, but I'm tired of pouring anguish on to a canvas. I want to do something hopeful and good. *That's* why I'm here. I know people will be talking about the accident again, but maybe this will shift their focus into thinking about Mom, Dad, and Teddy as people instead of about how they died. The only difference between you and me is that no one really *knows* how bad it's been for me."

Except for Cole. Because of last night, he knows.

Vanessa's eyes cloud over. "I'm sorry, Josie. I don't even want to be back in Castille, but I didn't have anywhere else to go. I'm surprised you *wanted* to come back."

"I wanted to come back for the mural, but also for you."

A faint light appears in her expression. She pats my hand. "I'm glad you did."

"So am I." Relief twines through my heart. "Hey, do you want to go shopping this weekend? Maybe we can have lunch, then pick up a few things for the baby. Are you going to decorate a nursery?"

"I haven't really thought about it." She sips her tea and shrugs. "I figured he'd just stay in my room."

"We can still get a nursery decorated. Paint, furniture, curtains." Warming to the idea, I check the calendar on my phone. "Let's plan for Saturday afternoon. I need a few things for the cottage too."

"I'm sorry I didn't have the cottage ready for you. Did the water and electricity work?"

"No, but Cole—"

My voice breaks off. I'm surprised at how easily his name still slides from my lips. Vanessa tenses.

"Cole?" she echoes.

I glance at her warily. The bad blood between all three of us runs in multiple directions.

"I saw him at the pier," I explain. "When I found out the electricity didn't work, he helped me out."

Her eyes ice over. "How?"

Discomfort rustles in my chest. "He let me stay overnight at his house."

"You mean his monstrous *estate* over on Sea Avenue? How did that happen?"

"I was in a bind last night." I swallow hard, unwilling to tell her about my panic attacks. "He happened to be there."

"You need to stay away from him." Vanessa sits back, folding her arms almost protectively around her belly. "He's not the man he used to be."

"I know." My unease intensifies. "I ran into Nathan Peterson this morning, and he gave me the lowdown on Cole's transformation into a corporate tycoon." I push to my feet and bring our cups to the sink. "I almost can't believe it."

"It's the truth. Nathan was the one who told me about it too, like he's the town herald warning people about the dragon." She gives a bitter laugh and shakes her head. "Cole Danforth, Castille's biggest tyrant. Can you imagine what Mom and Dad would say?"

I don't want to. Just the thought constricts my heart into a fist. I don't want to imagine what Mom and Dad would say about me and Vanessa either.

Ten years later, we're all so fucking *broken*.

Shaking off a sudden despondency, I turn back to my sister. "Hey, Nathan said he'd like to see you again. Didn't he have a huge crush on you in high school?"

She rolls her eyes, though a slight flush colors her cheeks. "Not to be conceited, but a lot of boys had a crush on me in high school."

"Well, he's always been really nice. Maybe you should go out with him."

"At seven months pregnant, you want me to go on a date with the police lieutenant?" Vanessa twists her mouth. "That would raise some eyebrows."

"Then you could give people lessons on how to pluck and shape them correctly."

She chuckles. "Starting with you, right?"

I grin, pleased by the resurgence of our teasing old camaraderie. Maybe there's hope yet.

"You want to check out the basement with me?" I ask.

"No, you go ahead." She waves to the basement door. "I'll take care of the dishes."

I head downstairs, flicking on the lights. The room is packed with cardboard boxes and plastic containers. My mother's paintings are stacked along the walls, and dropcloths cover her sculptures. My father's books teeter in piles on the old shelves.

A few boxes are scrawled with my name—items from the apartment I'd shared with Cole. Many of the boxes remain unopened. I hadn't wanted my old stuff.

I also don't want it all moldering here in my parents' basement. I should clear things out. I take a folder off the top of a box. My heart jumps. *Police Reports.*

These reports had been the only way I'd been able to illuminate the black hole in my memory. Cole had given his statement of events to the police, but I hadn't spoken to him after the night he left me. He hadn't been there to answer my endless questions, to help recreate the accident in my mind, to provide any light.

My hands shake. I open the folder. *Time and Location. Type of Accident. Name of Driver. Vehicle Type. Number of Persons Involved.*

The boxes are filled in with Chief Henry Peterson's scrawly black writing. Attached to the first page are several more typewritten sheets outlining the details of the investigation that the police had pieced together from Cole's statement, a timeline, and physical evidence.

I close the folder and set it aside. I'd read the report so many times I still have it memorized.

It had been raining when we left my parents' anniversary

party at the Seagull Inn. The clock was well past midnight. Both my parents had been drinking champagne, so Cole had offered to drive. I'd sat in the front passenger seat beside him, and my parents and Teddy rode in the back.

We should have arrived home twenty minutes later. Instead, just after Cole crossed the Old Mill Bridge on the coastal Highway 16, the SUV had skidded on a sharp turn. He'd been unable to correct course. The car had careened backward down the steep incline, crashing against a rock formation jutting into the ocean inlet. The velocity had crushed the back end like a tin can.

I'd blacked out. When I woke, I was in the hospital with Vanessa at my side, her eyes bloodshot and face streaked with tears. She told me I'd survived with a concussion and a broken arm. Cole sustained bruises and lacerations. Our parents and Teddy had been killed on impact.

The police reports detailed the events with factual detachment that I've tried to put in place of my lost memory. I'd read the reports over and over, hoping they would jar something loose.

How can I not remember the terror of a car careening out of control, the screech of skidding tires, the screams—surely there were screams—the stench of gasoline, the icy ocean water seeping through the doors?

Much later, long after Cole had left me, the investigation determined that he hadn't been speeding or under the influence. His cell phone showed no evidence of use while driving. The only explanation was that he might have been overtired owing to having worked long hours the previous night and the same day, but the police couldn't find anything obvious he might have done to stop the accident from happening.

The town, however, had swirled with rumors about Cole's wrongdoing. During my recovery, I'd heard them as if I were submerged underwater, listening to something I couldn't understand. After Cole left, I no longer cared what anyone said about him. I no longer cared about him.

The light had gone out on our relationship, once so filled with love and friendship. Nothing was left but the dark.

CHAPTER 7

Cole

I can't stop thinking about her. Her skin as pale as milk and her bright, leaf-green eyes. Her perfect bow-shaped mouth curved with the smile that never failed to lodge right into my heart. Straight dark hair falling to her shoulders, sometimes messy and tangled, sometimes pulled into a ponytail. Oversized T-shirt, torn jeans, boots streaked with paint.

A column of heat rises up my spine. No cloying perfume on her—only soap and shampoo that smelled like lemongrass. And the sweet scent of candy flavored with cherries and strawberries. She always picked the red ones. Red lip balm, red lollipop, red gummy bears, the red Lifesaver.

Her mismatched socks and bright red backpack. The way she nuzzled her nose into the space between my neck and shoulder. The slope of her hips, the breathy gasp in the back of her throat, the slide of her skin against mine. Her delight at opening a brand-new box of tissues with lotion. The way she—

"Knocked out another one like a bowling pin." Howard, one of the company publicists, puts his tablet on my office desk. "But not without a price."

"A good one." Forcing Josie out of my head, I shove the tablet back at him without looking at the screen. "Empire Scotch could never compete with Invicta, and they knew it."

My uncle Gerald grabs the tablet and scans the headline. *"Danforth drowns another small-batch craft distiller.* Nice."

I shrug. "They defaulted on their loan. Not my problem."

Gerald and Howard exchange wary looks. I stride to the map on my office wall. Dotted with color-coded pins, the map shows every single distiller of spirits across the United States, Mexico and Europe. The red pins indicate the Invicta Spirits holdings, many of which I've acquired since my father's death.

In addition to my own scotch whiskey, Invicta Spirits owns labels of gin, bourbon, rum, vodka, and brandy. Shiny unopened bottles of all our products line the glass shelves on the other side of the room. I've targeted a distillery in Mexico, marked with a blue pin on the map, to add tequila to our brands.

"In the past decade, I have pushed this company into the top tier of liquor producing companies in the whole fucking country." I fold my arms and stare at the map. "Pre-tax profits were up fifty percent last year. Turnover is pushing three quarters of a billion. And you think I'm worried about a *headline?*"

"The headline is just part of the problem." Howard shakes his head. "You may have won a legal battle in getting the zoning change and permit to expand the Fernsdown plant last year, but *no one* has forgotten that Danforth made zero concessions to the protesters."

"Or that you sent them a big fuck you by ignoring their requests to discuss their concerns about pollution, noise, and ordinance violations," Gerald adds. "Now in addition to controlling the Spring Hills well, you've pissed off the residents of Castille by forcing Blue River Water to shut down."

"I didn't force anything. They couldn't find an investor to save them."

"Because *you* blocked all potential interest," Howard says. "The residents loved that company's product and story. You *still* have a chance to soften the blow by hiring the folks who lost their jobs, but you need to move fast. The more time passes, the less people are willing to forgive."

I stare at the map again. I don't want *forgiveness*. And I don't want Invicta to be *one* of the top five liquor producing companies in the country. The only place for this company is at the top. Then I'll focus on expanding outside the country, taking on the biggest beverage companies in the world.

I pull a green pin off the map in northern New Hampshire and stick a red pin in its place. Another one down.

"We have software and analytics for that." His mouth twisting, Howard gestures to the map. "For a guy with a scorched-earth approach to business, your tracking system is pathetically old-school."

My shoulders tense. "I don't pay you to give me shit. Go away."

With a mutter of exasperation, he throws Gerald another pointed look and leaves.

"You pay your publicists to prevent you from destroying this company's image," Gerald snaps. "But it's a waste of damned money if you don't let them do their job. Even Machiavelli said a ruler has to do good *sometimes*. At least enough to keep the public from turning on you."

"He also said business is war."

"Wars have occasional truces," he retorts. "This is why we are sponsoring the Bicentennial Festival and why *you* are attending the events like you're a politician running for office. You will shake hands, smile, kiss babies, and act like you give a damn about the people of this town."

Even if you don't.

He doesn't have to say that.

Returning to the window overlooking Lantern Square, I sit at my desk. I'd turned the Snapdragon Inn into my personal office for two reasons—to get away from the constant questions, interruptions, and meetings at the main office and to remind Castille's residents that Cole Danforth isn't going anywhere.

"Next Saturday night." Gerald starts toward the door. "The fundraising dinner for the Arts Center. Bring someone who's reasonably well liked, like that girl Evelyn. People respected her father, so by association they might soften a little toward you. I wouldn't count on it, but stranger things have happened."

He heads out the door, slamming it behind him harder than he needs to. Much as my uncle's sensibility irritates me, it's one of the reasons I'd brought him onboard at Invicta. He'd been working for Hydrospace when I moved to New York after the accident, and he'd been the one to give me a foot in the door. A year after I started Invicta, Gerald left Hydrospace to join my company. Even then, he'd been the one person I could trust.

He still is. Guess that's why I keep him around. Even if he does give me constant shit about the way I run the business and my lack of concern about PR.

My father had been good at PR. A master, even. His tight friendships with the mayor, the chief of police, and the city council combined with his image as a fair, charismatic boss had hidden the fact that he was violent and abusive at home. Kevin Danforth, the man who'd funded a new social services building, would never have thrown a bottle of sleeping pills at his wife and told her to kill herself.

Of course not.

Fucking bastard. Let him rot in hell, even if that's still too good for him.

Swiveling my chair around, I gaze down at Lantern Square, five stories below my top-floor office. People are sitting in the plaza, eating lunch or drinking coffee, and pedestrians wander in and out of the four blocks of shops and restaurants surrounding the island.

Right beside the Snapdragon Inn, on a straight visual line to the left, are the Botanical Gardens, concealed by the wall where Josie thinks she'll be painting a mural of Castille's history.

The wall's proximity to my office is a thorn puncturing deep into my side. I'd be forced to see her every day until she finished, and then the mural itself would be a torturous reminder of both her and her parents. One I'd be confronted with every time I enter the office or look out the window.

Though I deserve the hit, I intend to stop her plan before she even gets started.

It's close to two. I take a file folder from my desk and walk to City Hall, where Allegra King has summoned me for the committee meeting about the festival. The company lawyers, publicists, and Gerald have been on my case for too long. If I help with the damned festival, maybe they'll finally shut up.

As I start up the steps, my spine tenses. I stop and turn.

Crossing the street toward me is Josie, carrying a large art portfolio. Her shoulder-length dark hair *bounces* like a shampoo ad. Faded jeans hug her legs and hips, and beneath her army jacket, her Grateful Dead T-shirt is just tight enough to show the curves of her tits.

Goddamn. I'm a teenager all over again, hard at the sight of her.

She glances both ways before crossing the street, then slows when she sees me.

"What are you doing here?" Her green eyes cloud with wariness.

"Meeting about the Bicentennial Festival. Invicta is sponsoring it."

"I heard."

She purses her lips. A protrusion appears in her cheek. Lifesaver? Jolly Rancher? She's still addicted. I drag my gaze to her mouth, the stain of red on her lower lip. She'd taste the same, sweet like cherries and strawberries. Sticky.

Heat rises to my chest. The taste of her had always gone right to my blood. I hadn't often been able to kiss her quickly and be done. I was greedy, impatient, wanting more. Sliding my lips from her sugary mouth to her smooth neck, stripping her clothes off, sucking on her pink berry-like nipples, her soft moan filling my head—

Clenching my teeth, I force myself to refocus. Last thing I need is to walk into the meeting with a raging hard-on.

Josie narrows her eyes. "I also heard you've morphed into an evil genius."

"You heard right."

Hurt, slight but unmistakable, crosses her features. I steel myself against it. I'm about to hurt her a lot worse.

"So is this sponsorship an attempt to revamp your hardcore image?" she asks.

"According to my PR people and my uncle, yes." I reach past her to open the door. She passes me in a rush of cool, good-smelling air.

"And according to you?"

She starts toward the main conference room. As I expected, she's going to the same meeting. Good. Time to put an end to this.

"I don't care about my image."

"Yeah, that's why you wear fifteen-thousand dollar watches and tailored suits." She throws me a derisive look before striding into the conference room.

Allegra and several members of both the city council and the festival committee are gathered around the table. With tangible surprise, they glance from me to Josie and back again as if not sure how to deal with this.

Allegra's brow furrows. She crosses the room, putting herself between me and Josie. She says something to Josie in a low tone.

Josie shakes her head and responds with a faint but reassuring smile. Then Allegra approaches me, her features set.

"I owe you an apology." Narrowing her eyes, she glances back at Josie. "I wasn't thinking when I asked you to be here. I'd forgotten that David...he's the head of the festival committee... had also asked Josie to attend."

"It doesn't matter."

"That's what she said, but I want you to know it wasn't intentional."

"Sure."

She rolls her eyes slightly in exasperation, then returns to her seat. "If you would both please sit down, we'll get started right away."

Josie and I sit at opposite ends of the table. Tension thickens the air. The meeting begins. It's a mind-numbing discussion of the festival events—concerts on the square, food booths, an open-air Night Market, a kids' art exhibit, a dog festival at Central Bark. At the center of the activities are the parade and the unveiling of the Lantern Square mural.

Or not. For now, I keep my mouth shut.

"Josie, we're anxious to see your design," Allegra says.

Josie takes two poster boards from her portfolio and sets them on a stand at the front of the room. In her intricate, unmistakable style is a sweeping scene of Castille, with the ocean crossing the foreground.

"The proposal for a mural about the history of Castille is almost a decade old," she explains. "Shortly after the accident, Castille Elementary created a memorial garden for my brother, but the mural proposal for my parents was never completed. I want to change that, both in their memory and for Castille. One of my father's favorite quotes was from the historian David McCullough. *'History is who we are and why we are the way we are.'* Castille is a huge part of who I am. Of all of us. But when I think about this town, the first thing that comes to mind is the ocean."

She indicates the drawings. "I think about the lobster boats leaving the cove at the crack of dawn. I think about fishing on Marlett's Shore, biking on the coastal trail by the lighthouse, hanging out at the pier. I think about swimming at Hyde Beach, the freezing cold water and the blazing sun. And when I was creating this design, I realized that the ocean is a major part of Castille's history and mine. It's a constant. The one thing that hasn't changed."

She pauses. Her slender throat works with a swallow. I clench my jaw, my insides tightening.

Josie spreads her hand over the white-capped ocean in the foreground, rendered as an underwater view laden with fish and plants. "I envision the mural as the history of the town, starting with Native American and First Nation people, then the colonial era and continuing until today. The ocean is at the forefront, the element that has shaped the town more powerfully than anything else."

The committee members all murmur with impressed approval. Josie hands out bound folders with details of her concepts, including a section about color and paint type.

"Since arriving several days ago, I've looked at the wall and surrounding space more closely," she continues. "I've also taken into consideration the fact that the wall is next to the Botanical Gardens. I plan to use a specific color palette and light effects so the art reflects the unity of the ocean, the gardens, and the town. I'll use a matte acrylic paint tinted with raw pigment, which will give the entire wall the soft aesthetic of a fresco. This will also contribute to both the natural and historical feeling of the work."

An old hard pride in her talent floods my chest. I smother it.

With growing pleasure, the committee members study the drawings and ask Josie questions about the subject and technique.

"This is wonderful," Allegra says. "That wall has needed a

facelift for ages, and this is the perfect solution. I'm delighted you approached us with the proposal."

"We've already budgeted for the paint and scaffolding." John Porter, vice-president of the Historical Society and a man who'd been a close friend of Benjamin Mays, hands Josie a budget sheet. "If you could let us know what else you need, that will help us going forward."

"And you can get this done by August tenth?" Miriam, the Castille Museum director, asks. "The plans for the festival are well underway, and we'd like to unveil the mural in the morning so people can enjoy it for the rest of the day."

Josie nods. "I need to finalize my sketches, but yes. I'll make the deadline."

"Invicta Spirits is our main sponsor of the festival." Allegra gives me a tight smile. "I've asked Mr. Danforth to be present so he can give us further ideas about his company's role."

Avoiding Josie's gaze, I open my folder and pass a stack of printed papers to my right.

"Much as I appreciate the effort to beautify Lantern Square," I say, "I need to point out that the mural is prohibited based on municipal city code ordinance 105.54B."

A tense hush falls over the room.

"The ordinance only allows murals on private property, and with strict regulations." I tap a forefinger on the paper. "It also groups murals *not* on private property in the same category as graffiti, which is illegal vandalism punishable by both a fine and possible jail time."

Silence. Josie's shocked glare spears into my chest like a harpoon.

"That is the most ridiculous thing I've ever heard." Allegra tosses the paper onto the table, anger sparking in her eyes. "This *work of art* is the exact opposite of graffiti."

"It's still city code. There's also the matter of the historical preservation ordinance, which likewise prohibits murals on or in the vicinity of historic property. The wall enclosing the Botanical Gardens was built shortly after the garden itself was constructed, dating it to the late nineteenth century."

"A wall is not a historic building," Miriam snaps.

"I'm sure the Historical Society would disagree."

Another silence stretches. They study the code print-outs I'd given them. I feel Josie's anger like a living thing. I can't look at her.

"We'll get this fixed next week." Allegra sweeps her gaze around the room with a sharp nod of satisfaction. "Ordinances can't be amended overnight, but we can start the process right away. Everyone is in favor of the mural being painted on the garden wall."

"What about the property owner?" I ask.

"The property owner?" Miriam pulls her eyebrows together. "The city owns the property."

"The city owns the Botanical Gardens," I correct. "Not the masonry section of the wall."

"What in the love of God are you talking about now?" Allegra snaps. "Josie, I apologize for this interruption."

"On page three, you'll see the zoning and parcel map for the Snapdragon Inn, which I purchased five years ago," I continue. "The southeast corner of the property extends past the boundary of the garden wall. History will attest to the fact that when the gardens were constructed, the owner of the Snapdragon Inn, a Mr. Charles Buckham, sought to block any potential noise or crowding that might disturb his guests. To that end, he constructed the wall separating the gardens from his property lot."

"What is the point of this?" Allegra pinches the bridge of her nose in exasperation.

"The point is that I am the legal owner of the garden wall. The masonry section is within the boundaries of the lot I purchased.

Murals on private property are allowed only with express permission of the owner."

Josie plants her hands on the table, leaning forward to skewer me with a glare. "Then give me permission."

"No."

She pales, disbelief flashing in her eyes. "This is for my *parents*."

Fuck. Pain splinters in my chest. I submerge it beneath a layer of ice and shake my head.

"I will not give you permission." Gripping the edge of the table, I force myself to meet her gaze. "If you go through with this project, you'll be in violation of the law."

She stares at me like she's never seen me before. The air crackles between us, lit with her fire.

"I intend to verify all this with the city assessor's office." Allegra grabs the folder and rises to her feet. "Ladies and gentlemen, I apologize for this unpleasant wrench in the works. Josie, rest assured I will get to the bottom of this immediately. Meeting adjourned."

She throws me a withering scowl and stalks out of the room. Josie stuffs her drawings back into her portfolio and follows, her shoulders set.

Sweat trickles down my neck. Every muscle in my body is locked. I grab the empty folder and leave the room.

CHAPTER 8

Cole

The early summer air does nothing to ease the burn. I lock my office door before sitting down to work. I've trained myself to be single-minded and analytical about budgets, acquisitions, and expansion. I've learned to make decisions fast and execute them with as little compromise as possible. No warning either. The little craft distilleries and Blue River never knew what hit them.

It should have been easier to blindside Josie the same way.

"Sir?" The security guard phones in from downstairs. "There's a woman here insisting she needs to speak with you."

"Name?"

"Josephine Mays."

"Let her in."

I turn off the intercom and unlock my office door. A few minutes pass before the door flies open. Josie barges in, her hands fisted and an angry light in her eyes.

"You are an asshole," she snaps.

"I've been told."

"How dare you pull that kind of stunt?"

"It's the truth."

"And we both know damned well you brought it up only because *I'm* involved." She tosses her backpack and art portfolio onto a chair. She's trembling with anger. "I don't care what you think about me, but bringing the people of this town into our personal shit is low, even for you."

My shoulders tense. "*Even* for me? What do you know about me?"

"Nothing anymore." She slams her hands to her hips, her features twisting. "But I used to know *everything* about you. Do you remember that? Then you walked out on me right when I needed you the most, proving you were never the man I thought you were. Now I find out that you run this company like a dictator, you're crushing independent businesses and putting people out of work, and you're publicly trying to stop me from creating a mural that's intended for both this town and my parents. What the *hell* happened to you?"

"*You* happened to me."

The words fly out of my mouth before I can stop them. The pencil I'm holding breaks in two with the force of my grip.

Josie steps back, her eyes widening. Her dark hair is windblown, her cheeks flushed, her chest heaving under her old army jacket. I'd once had the right to comb her hair back from her forehead, slide my palm over her neck before edging my fingers into her V-necked T-shirt...

Anger crushes my chest. I shove away from my desk and stride toward her. Fear flashes in her green eyes, which pisses me off even more. When the fuck was she ever afraid of me?

I grab the lapels of her jacket, yanking her closer. Our lower bodies collide. She gasps, a little catching noise in the back of her throat that used to get me hot in a second.

It still does. My blood starts to boil. She tilts her head back, her eyes flashing. I lower my head to look at her, fighting to ignore her scent—goddamned summer leaves and cherry candy.

"I once would have done anything for you." The words grate roughly from my throat. "And then I failed you in the worst possible way. I failed you, I failed Teddy, and I failed your parents."

She stares at me, her breath hitching. "Cole, I—"

"When you left, I hoped with everything I was that you'd have a chance at a normal life." I pull her closer, anger warring with the undeniable flare of lust. "That you could be happy again if you weren't constantly surrounded by reminders of everything you lost. Everything *I took from you*."

"Goddamn you, Cole Danforth." Fire flames over her expression. She plants her hands on my chest and shoves herself away. "The only thing you *took* from me was *you*. That is the only way you failed me. When you walked out that door, I lost any chance of happiness or healing. So don't you fucking dare think you can push me away again by stopping me from doing what I came here to do."

I clench my teeth. My breath burns my lungs.

Lost any chance.

Holy shit. What have I done to her? I failed her in more ways than I can count, for longer than I'd ever imagined. Nothing I've done has worked to protect her. The girl I'd once loved more than life. I can't fail her again. *Won't.*

"And it doesn't look like the past ten years have worked out well for you either." She extends her arm to the view of Lantern Square. "Yeah, you're a big shot now. But throwing your weight around and crushing other businesses for revenge on this town? That's not something the Cole Danforth *I* used to know would do."

"I'm not the Cole Danforth you used to know."

Pain darkens her eyes. "And you have no idea how much that breaks my heart."

Curses lash through my brain. I stare at her—flushed skin, her perfect mouth tight with anger, her fire-green eyes. I might not be able to drive her away from Castille. But I sure as hell can drive her away from *me*.

After stalking across the room, I grab her shoulders. I lower my head and pull her closer at the same time. Crush my mouth to hers.

Oh fuck.

My head spins. Her gasp melts on my tongue. My chest constricts. She's everything I remember and more—ripe cherries and whipped cream. Fireflies. Waterfalls. Cotton candy.

She presses her body into mine, arching forward, her curves fitting against my chest. Heat fires my veins. I clutch her hips, pushing my tongue into her mouth, drinking her in. She tenses, then parts her lips wider, tangling her tongue with mine. So damned sweet.

Pressure collects at the base of my spine. Blood pulses in my dick. She drives her other hand into my hair and tugs me closer. Images flash in my head—Josie naked and writhing underneath me, grabbing my hair, her breathy cries filling my ears. Locking her legs around my hips, letting me thrust into her so deep…

The world tilts. It's like the first hit of a drug, all-consuming and addictive, driving the urgent craving for more. More. Fucking *more*.

Pulling her head back, I devour her perfect mouth. I push my hand up the back of her T-shirt. Stroke my fingers over the hot curve of her lower back. She flinches, her grip tightening in my hair, her breath increasing.

Then she moans, a soft little sound like she used to make when I woke her from a deep sleep, and rubs her breasts against my chest. I want to rip her clothes off, spread her legs, thrust into

her so hard she'll never again doubt that she will always belong
to me.

Scare her away.

Tension claws at my insides. I trail my lips over her cheek to
her ear, dragging in a heavy breath. Her hair smells like strawberries.

Scare her, you stupid fuck.

I tighten my hands on her waist and push her backward. She
stumbles, her back coming up against the wall. Her eyes widen.
Fire flares in my blood. I shove my hand between her legs and
press hard. Gripping her throat, I slant my mouth over hers and
pinion her to the wall. Tension vibrates through her, even as she
clenches her thighs around my hand.

"Been awhile for you, huh, Josie?" I drag my teeth over her
lower lip. "No wonder you're so fired up. You still get yourself off
the same way or do you have new techniques now?"

She yanks her head back, her eyes burning. "Goddamn you."

I smile. "Too late."

Grabbing my shirt, she shoves me away and stalks past me to
pick up her backpack. "I mean it. You're an asshole."

I drag in a breath, trying to smother the heat still boiling in
my blood.

"I told you I don't want you here," I reply coldly. "But if it's a
fuck you're after, I'm happy to oblige."

"I'll keep that in mind." The lines of her body tense. Her eyes
spit fire at me. "Hate-fucking was never my style, but there's a
first time for everything."

Pushing her hair away from her face, she heads to the door.
Just before opening it, she turns back to face me.

"I came back to do something good here." Her jaw clenches.
"It makes me sick that you, of all people, want to stop me." She
shakes her head, pressing her lips together. "I'm so fucking disap-
pointed in you."

The words hit the middle of my chest like a blow, robbing my breath. She leaves, shutting the door hard behind her.

I sink into a chair, resting my head in my hands. Fear burns low in my gut.

When I was eleven, I had very few defenses against Josie Mays. Now, at thirty-three, I have none. She demolished them with one look.

That right there could be my downfall.

CHAPTER 9

Josie

I *should have known.*

I did know, but I haven't wanted to acknowledge it. One touch of Cole's mouth and one press of his hand, and my body reacted as if it were a dry leaf going up in flames. Even though he's drastically changed, he's still imprinted on me, in my very cells. I still want him on a visceral, primal level ruled by instinct rather than logic and clear thinking.

I turn my face to the shower spray and close my eyes as sensations pulse through my blood. My fantasies about Cole have always been exceptionally vivid, intensified by my memory that everything I think about had once been so *real*.

And now...

Pulling in a breath, I turn off the shower and step out. Though I'm pissed off that Cole's angry kiss yesterday actually turned me on, I cut myself some slack. I haven't even been kissed, much less had sex, in well over a year and a half. It's hardly a wonder that a hot encounter aroused me to the breaking point. Even with him.

Especially with him.

After drying myself off, I get dressed, slipping the evil-eye amulet into my pocket. I try to stop thinking about Cole, focusing instead on what I have to do next to get the mural painted. I've spent the morning on the phone discussing options with city council members, though no alternate plan has been reached.

"I've been involved in Castille government for years," Allegra King had told me. "I can honestly tell you I don't remember a single time we've had to address the city's mural code. I was unacceptably remiss in not looking into it in more depth when I received your proposal."

Since Allegra has never struck me as a woman who is anything less than scrupulous, I suspect she's politely taking the blame for something that was the responsibility of a City Hall subordinate.

Not that anyone except big bad Cole Danforth should be *blamed*.

At two, I walk downtown to meet Vanessa, who is waiting for me beside her car near the courthouse. Her rusted old Dodge looks as if it was salvaged from a junkyard.

"All I could afford after my bastard ex took off." Noticing me eyeing the car, she gives me a wry smile. "But at least it runs."

I dislike the idea of her driving such a junk heap while she's seven months pregnant. And what about when the baby is born? No way does this car have all the necessary safety features for a car seat.

Since our relationship is still on tentative ground, I keep my mouth shut for now but plan to strategize about how I can help her get a new car. We head to the shops, stopping to visit several home goods stores and baby boutiques. I tell her about the meeting and Cole's blockade of the mural.

"Given his asshole reputation, I'm not surprised." She takes a baby-blue infant jumpsuit off the rack and holds it up. "But there are plenty of other places in town where you can paint the mural. It's not as if the garden wall is the only place."

"I know, but that's not the entire point." I run my hand over a plush rocking horse in the center of the baby boutique. "If I paint it on city property, there's some sort of mural ordinance that has to be dealt with. Whereas if Cole would stop being a jerk and give me permission, I could get started right away. And there's definitely no other suitable wall in Lantern Square, which is the oldest and most popular part of town. The mural was supposed to be in the heart of downtown. Now Allegra is scrambling to try and find another location."

Guilt twinges in my chest. I hate knowing I'm putting both Allegra and the committee members in a bad position. The announcement for the mural unveiling has already been printed in the Bicentennial Festival program, and everyone has been apologizing to *me*, as if the garden wall debacle is their fault rather than an asinine blockade by Tycoon Cole.

"Have you talked to Cole directly?" Vanessa shifts her attention to a shelf filled with baby booties. "Not that he'd budge."

I examine an embroidered pillow, hoping she doesn't notice the warmth rising to my cheeks. Yeah, I've *talked* to him. I've also done other things with him.

Ugh. My lips still tingle from his kiss, the delicious scrape of his stubble. Not in all our years together had he ever kissed me quite like that. And we'd kissed an awful lot.

"He wasn't very responsive." *Well, isn't that a colossal lie?* I'd felt Cole's big hard response right up against my belly.

My flush deepens. That kiss has seared through me like a bolt of fire, sizzling my nerves and demolishing my defenses. My lips, my body, my heart...everything had remembered him with the power of a thousand shooting stars, as if all our years apart had converged into that one moment.

And *then*…

Much as I hate his cruelty, part of me reluctantly understands. The view from Cole's office window includes the entire wall of the Botanical Gardens. He would only have to glance out the window to see the mural, which for him would be another soul-searing reminder of the accident. Of his belief that he failed me.

But what about the town of Castille *doesn't* serve as a reminder of all that we once had? Peddler's Ice Cream Shop, Ford's College, the cafés we'd frequented, the acres of woodlands, the ocean, the pier…This whole town is our memory book.

But Cole *chose* to come back here. Even if his reasons were for mafia-level revenge over his father and the town that failed him and his mother…like me, Castille must still hold good memories for him. This is where we met. Where we climbed trees, swam at the beach, leapt together off Eagle Cliff. This is where we fell in love.

Does he ever think of those times? Or was our entire past obliterated that horrible night?

I set the pillow down and refocus my brain. "Have you thought about nursery colors yet?"

Vanessa touches a baby blanket patterned with ducklings. "I know blue is a cliché for a boy, but it's my favorite color. Blue and cream, maybe with an ocean theme."

"That's a great idea. I could paint some animals on the wall, if you want. A whale, seahorses, plants."

She smiles, which turns her face from pretty to beautiful. "That would be really nice."

Enthused by the idea, I pull several children's picture books about fish and whales from a nearby shelf. I can create an entire underwater theme with a little submarine, a pirate's treasure chest, and all different kinds of sea animals. Octopi, smiling clown fish, pufferfish, sharks…

I leaf through a photography book featuring stunning color photos of marine life and waves rolling over sand and tide pools.

I gaze at a photo of a rocky inlet, a mist of spray crashing against the shore.

I haven't had a chance to visit the ocean yet. I can also make a trip to the aquarium to see the—

Sudden cold prickles my skin. An image takes shape in my head—a ghostly pale face submerged in freezing water, blood pluming around the distorted features and ice-blue eyes, mouth contorted...

Holy shit.

Panic flares. My lungs constrict. *I can't breathe. I'm drowning.*

I grab the shelf, forcing myself to feel the ground under my feet, the solidity of the book in my hand. Lullaby music drifts from the store's speakers. Closing my eyes, I drag in a breath and slip my hand into my pocket, unconsciously gripping the silver amulet.

Evil eyes. That's what I've been seeing all this time. Haunted, vacant, demonic. They've been cursing me.

"What do you think of this one?" My sister's voice eases the tightness in my chest.

Suppressing the fear, I set the book back on the shelf and turn. Vanessa is holding up an ocean-patterned bedding set. I nod with approval.

"There's also a stuffed Nemo." I try to dismiss the horrible image, but it lingers like a ghost.

Nightmares. I've only ever seen the disembodied heads during my shallow sleep. Not in the daylight, and certainly not while surrounded by soft baby clothes and colorful picture books.

I wipe a trickle of sweat from my temple. *Good things. New nephew. Hope for the future.*

I take the crib bedding and stuffed Nemo to the cash register.

"You don't have to buy that, Josie." Vanessa follows me.

"Yes, I do." Well aware that she's in financial straits, I hand the cashier my credit card. "More importantly, I want to."

We spend the next hour shopping. I buy two lamps and

several spare bulbs for the cottage. Though I've been fine there so far, these hallucinations I've had during the day won't make it easier to contend with nighttime. The more light I have, the better.

As dusk approaches, Vanessa and I have dinner at a Mediterranean café, discussing my career and her recent trip to Portland. By the time we pay the bill, our enjoyable few hours together has mitigated my lingering unease.

We return to her car and put several shopping bags in the trunk.

"Do you want a ride home?" she asks.

"No, I'll walk. It's a nice night, and I could use a little exercise after that dessert."

"Evening, ladies." Nathan Peterson approaches from his parked patrol car, glancing at the Dodge. "You sure that thing is safe?"

"I just use it to get around town." Two spots of color appear on Vanessa's cheeks as she closes the trunk.

"I have a friend who's a mechanic." Nathan's brow furrows. "I can take it over to have him check it out, make sure the engine is okay."

"No need, but thank you." Vanessa takes her keys out of her purse and steps away from him.

Sensing my sister's unease, I give Nathan a bright smile. "What are you up to this evening, Officer Peterson?"

"Usual patrol." A frown darkens his face. "I heard about what Danforth did to you at the meeting. I'm sorry you have to deal with this kind of crap."

"So am I, but I'll figure it out."

"Hey, are you both going to the Arts Center fundraiser next weekend?" He glances at Vanessa again. "It's a dinner-dance and silent auction over at the country club."

I shake my head. "Not me."

"Me either." Vanessa opens the car door.

"If you'd like to go, I'd be happy to take you." Nathan appears to be talking to both of us, but his gaze stays squarely on Vanessa. "I know a lot of people there would like to see you."

Hesitation rises to her expression. I get it. Neither of us are thrilled at the idea of facing a crowd of people who might very well look at us with pity. But Vanessa is the one who will still be living here after I've left, and Nathan is looking at her with such hope....

"Why don't you two go?" I reach into the backseat to pick up a paper bag containing the two lamps I'd bought earlier. "I'm still busy getting settled in, but it sounds like it'd be a lot of fun for you."

My sister shoots me a narrow look. "I'm not really up for socializing."

"We can just go for an hour or so," Nathan suggests. "Or we can leave whenever you want."

"No, thanks." Vanessa gets into her car, adjusting the seatbelt around her belly. "See you both later."

She closes the door. The car starts with a rattle, belching out a stream of exhaust. Nathan and I both watch as she drives away.

Disappointment nudges at me. Vanessa doesn't have any friends left in town—or if she does, she doesn't want to associate with them right now—but Nathan has always liked her. She couldn't have a better *first friend* than him.

Maybe even a romantic one. I think she needs light and hope as much as I do. *As much as Cole does.*

"You want me to talk to my mechanic friend?" Nathan asks. "He might have some leads on a decent used car."

"That would be great, thanks. I'd like to help her find something more reliable." I point my thumb toward the path leading to the harbor. "I'll see you later. I'm heading back to the cottage."

He pulls his eyebrows together. "We've had a few problems with vagrants up on the hill. You shouldn't walk up there alone."

Great. Another thing I need to be freaked out about.

"I'll be okay." I pat my backpack. "I have a really good flashlight."

"I can go with you." He glances at his watch and reaches out to take the bag from me. "My shift is about over."

Given his warning, I decide walking home with a police officer in uniform is not a bad idea. We head back to the cove and up the hill. I unlock the cottage door and usher him inside.

"Nice place." Putting the bag down, Nathan looks around the sunroom appreciatively. "I've never been here."

"My mother used it as a studio." I set one of the lamps on a rickety little table beside the sofa and the other near my easel. "Vanessa said she'll help me decorate it."

"She's back into interior design?"

"I hope so. She was so good at it." Sorrow flickers through me. My sister's talent was yet another thing lost in the decade-long darkness following the accident. "Maybe decorating this place will give her ideas about how she can start again. Hey, can I offer you something to drink?"

"I'll take a soda, if you have one."

"Sure. Have a seat." I fill two glasses with ice and pour us each a soda.

He settles on the sofa in front of the picture window. The sun making its final descent over the cove is a lovely picture of reddish gold light. I'm probably the only person in the world who doesn't love sunsets. After sunset comes the dark.

"That's yours, huh?" Nathan nods to the small easel.

"Yeah, but I haven't come up with any ideas for what to paint yet." I keep hoping I'll be inspired to paint something good. Hopeful. Hell, I'd even settle for *pretty*. Anything but a horror show.

"Looks like you have a picture right here." He gestures to the view.

"I'm already painting Castille for the mural." I sit on a chair beside him and look at the blank canvas.

I used to love creating my whimsical, detailed little creatures, all scientifically precise with settings often influenced by Dutch genre paintings. While my mother's art had been big and expansive—mystical images of women bursting with color and light— my paintings were smaller and quieter. I'd wanted the viewer to connect with my work on a personal, intimate level, the way a reader connects with a beloved book.

Whimsy and personal intimacy are no longer my aesthetic. I don't know what is.

"Did you know Ms. Havers still teaches art over at the high school?" Nathan takes a gulp of soda.

"Yes." I smile at the thought of my favorite teacher. "I'm hoping to visit her soon."

"She married Mr. Larson from the middle school," Nathan says. "He taught sixth grade and had this really impressive moustache that he agreed to shave off one year if the school met the fundraising goal."

"I remember that. It was a handlebar moustache." Fondness rises in me. I have plenty of good memories about Castille. I just need to be reminded of them.

Nathan and I spend the next hour reminiscing, and his easygoing company is a welcome reprieve. He takes his empty glass to the sink, pausing to reach for mine. As I glance up at him, my heart suddenly jumps into my throat.

Nathan's face looking down at me. Angular cheekbones, wide horrified eyes, blood pooling on his skin...

"Hey, you okay?"

His voice breaks through my shock. I hand him the glass, fighting to school my expression into one of calm.

"Yes, sorry." I manage a small laugh. All I need is for the police lieutenant to think I'm crazy. "Sometimes I get these...um, flashes of strange things. Post-traumatic stress related."

"What kind of strange things?"

"Disembodied heads, usually." I twist my mouth wryly. "In the past few years they've made their way into my art. My last series sold out, if you can believe that."

"Actually I can." He sets the glasses in the sink. "People like scary stuff. That's why horror movies are so popular."

"I'd rather paint flowers." I rise, rubbing my palms together.

That's not strictly true, though. I do want to create provocative art that challenges people, but not in a horrible, shocking way. My mother had pushed boundaries and made statements through incredible paintings that glowed with life, not death. Surely I can do the same thing.

"I should get going." Nathan picks up his lightweight jacket from the sofa. "It was good seeing you again."

"You too." I walk him to the entryway. "Maybe we—"

A knock suddenly rattles the door. Nathan frowns. "You expecting someone?"

"No." I peer through the peephole. The porch light doesn't work, but I catch a glimpse of Cole's set features. My heart slams against my chest.

Wary, I open the door. "What are you doing here?"

The sheer impact of his presence jolts me to the core. Sunset light creates golden streaks on his hair. A faded *Montreal Canadiens* T-shirt clings to his chest and shoulders, and worn jeans hug his muscular legs. Everything inside me weakens.

Back when we were together, he'd worn a suit and tie a few times, but even then I'd preferred him in jeans with his hair messy and jaw scratchy with stubble. It had always been so easy to slide my hands under his T-shirt, seeking out the smooth ridges of his abdomen and—

Stop it.

He slants his gaze narrowly to Nathan. "What's *he* doing here?"

The two men lock stares. Tension seizes the air.

This should be fun.

In high school, the two of them hadn't been friendly—

Nathan's father had been the chief of police, a man known for being chummy with Kevin Danforth—but as far as I know, Cole and Nathan had chosen to ignore each other rather than engage in open dislike. However, after what Cole did to Nathan's brother and his bottled water company, that appears to have changed.

"Josie and I are old friends." Nathan rests his hand with deceptive casualness on his gun.

I glance uneasily between them. "Cole helped me out with some repairs when I got here. The electricity hadn't been turned on."

"You should have called the police department." Nathan keeps his steel-edged gaze on Cole. "We'd have helped you out."

"Cole, what are you doing here?" I repeat, stepping partway between them.

He indicates my portfolio, which I hadn't realized he was holding. "You left this in my office."

"Thank you." I take the portfolio from him, suppressing a shiver when our fingers brush.

"I'll change this." He points to the burned-out porch light. "The contractor left some extra bulbs. No need to stay, Officer Peterson."

He tilts his chin at Nathan. A distinct territorial vibe radiates from Cole, one I don't like at all. Yes, he'd come to my rescue last week, but he's being an ass about the mural and trying to bully me into leaving.

That aside, he has no right to be possessive about me because I'm definitely no longer *his*. Even if his kiss had gotten me so fired up I'd throbbed.

"I'll stay," Nathan says decisively.

My stomach knots. I'm not about to get caught in the middle of some pissing contest between the town villain and the chief law-enforcement officer.

I pull the door open wider. "Thanks for your help, Nathan, but I'll be fine."

He frowns. "You sure?"

"I'm sure." Not wanting Cole to think he *won*, I add, "I'll swing by the department later this week. Maybe you, me, and Vanessa can get together for dinner."

"I'd like that." Shooting Cole another glare, Nathan steps toward the door. "Take care, Josie. Just call if you need anything."

He and Cole face off in the doorway, neither one stepping aside to let the other pass. Finally Nathan backs down. Cole strides past him into the sunroom as if he owns the place. I say goodbye to Nathan and set my portfolio on a chair, suddenly questioning the wisdom of being alone with Cole again.

He stalks into the kitchen, casting a cursory glance over the clutter—my easel and paints, a sweatshirt thrown over the sofa, books piled on the wooden crate I'm using as a coffee table. I can almost see the judgments forming in his brain. When we lived together, my scattered disorganization had been an occasional source of contention. As had his penchant for over-cleaning and throwing things out.

He closes the storage closet and returns to the porch with the lightbulb. As he reaches to unscrew the old bulb, his T-shirt rides up. My gaze snaps to the exposed ridges of his abdomen.

"That the first time you've seen Peterson?" Tension threads Cole's shoulders.

"No. Vanessa and I were just doing some shopping downtown. Nathan happened to be there."

"Stay away from him."

"Really?" Irritation ripples down my spine. "You think you have a right to give me an order?"

"It's a warning."

A warning. Cold ices my blood. Twice now, I've had odd images of Nathan's pale face and red eyes.

Don't be silly. They were hallucinations, like the ones you've had before that ended up on canvas. The ones that finally drove you back here.

"You're the one who should come with a warning," I say tartly. "I heard you shut down Richard Peterson's bottled water company. And not in a good way."

Cole flips on the porch light and closes the door. "His fault for defaulting on the loan."

"And *revenge* had nothing to do with it?"

His jaw tightens. "Richard Peterson was a goddamned bully who was bottling groundwater from three locations near former human waste and petroleum dump sites and selling it...way over-priced...as pure spring water. His company deserved to be shut down as much as the Iron Horse did."

I blink, startled by this different side to the story. "Then why does everyone think you're so..."

Terrible?

Painful understanding snaps inside me like a lock clicking into place. As a teenager, even as a child, Cole had had a reputa-tion for being a troublemaker and a bad kid. No one had believed his accusations of abuse against his charismatic, successful father. No one had believed Cole was capable of *good*. The accident had only intensified the town's negative view of him.

So many drastic changes in our lives. And yet that one thing has remained the same.

I'd once been the only person who'd known there was more to him. The quiet boy who brought me my forgotten backpack, returned my dropped roll of Lifesavers, left my stuffed rabbit Wally on the front porch after I'd lost him in the woods, saved my Halloween candy...to me, Cole Danforth was mysterious, fascinating, and heroic. Everyone else had it all wrong.

And now he's embodied his bad reputation on a whole other level.

An ache constricts my throat. "Nathan told me eighty people were left unemployed by the shutdown."

"And that's my fault?" He strides to the sunroom. "I'm not in the business of hiring everyone who loses their job because of their shitty employer. I'm not a crusader in disguise either. I don't shut down lousy companies for the greater good. Peterson was duping his customers, but you're damned right I was out for revenge. It was a sheer pleasure watching him fall. I'd waited my whole life to take down my father's company too. But I don't do a damned fucking thing if I don't think I'm going to make a profit. Because of that, Invicta Spirits will soon be the top liquor producing company in the country."

"Then you'll take on the world, right?" Disappointment, sharp and acute, lances through my chest.

Over the past decade, my pain mutated into nightmares and phobias. His turned into ruthless ambition. Which one is worse?

"Stop looking at me like that." His expression suddenly darkens.

"Like what?"

"Like you lost your best friend," he snaps.

"I *did*." Unexpected tears sting my eyes. "Ten years ago."

He stares at me, his face paling beneath his tan. A live wire of tension crackles in the air and arcs right into my blood.

"Goddammit, Josie." He turns away, his shoulders stiff.

I grab my portfolio and unzip it. My hands tremble. Years ago Cole and I stood on a cliff at Eagle Canyon, both of us drenched by the sun and vibrating with the awareness of what we could be together. I'd known in that instant that whatever happened *next* would change everything between us.

I have that instinct again now.

"I want to show you something." Shuffling through my artwork, I pull out my preliminary drawings for the mural and spread them out on the bed. "Look at these."

He glances at the drawings, his fists clenched. "I saw them already."

"No. *Look* at them." I step back, willing him not to block me out again.

The moment stretches. Finally he moves to the bed, his hands on his hips. He stares at the drawings. Deep lines groove his forehead.

I know the second he sees it. The rigid line of his profile softens ever so slightly. He expels a breath, his shoulders slumping.

"Castille has a history of its own." I walk to his side. "But so do I. So do *we*."

He studies the images, the woodlands stretching between the lighthouse and downtown. Nestled in the branches of a pine is a platform treehouse with a dangling rope for climbing. On the Water's Edge Pier, two carnival-goers sit astride the goofy whale on the Ocean Carousel. A tall young man with sun-streaked brown hair staffs the Milk Bottle Toss game booth. Far in the distance, where Eagle River cuts and twists through the canyon, that same man stands on the cliff, his arms outstretched, poised to leap.

"I've spent a lot of energy these past ten years being angry with you." The old ache of loss spreads through me, dark and empty. "I've come to some understanding about why you left, but mostly it's just been a wasteland. I'm tired of fear and darkness. I'm really tired of nightmares and not remembering.

"And I'm tired of resenting you, hating what you did, being angry. I came back to see if I could *somehow* come to terms with what happened. I'm trying to close the distance between me and my sister. I'm trying to put something good into the world with the mural. And you can bluster around all you want, but you forget that I once *knew* you. I still know things about you."

A muscle jumps in his jaw, the only evidence past his implacable expression that he's even listening.

"I know your Monopoly strategy of developing your proper-ties really fast," I continue. "I know you can't stand shirts with tags and that you sprained your wrist when you were thirteen attempting a one-handed cartwheel. I know you always go to McGinty's pub on the first day of hockey season. I know you're

Team Superman, that you don't like mushrooms, and that you have a birthmark shaped like an arrow right above your butt. I know Magus was your favorite character on *Empire of the Gods* and that your mother's father was the one who introduced you to Marine Sciences. I know the best cake I've ever eaten was the lemon cake you made for my twentieth birthday. I know you would never hate-fuck me."

Darkness flashes in his eyes. He shakes his head and turns to the door. My heart sinks to the pit of my stomach. If the evidence of what we once meant to each other isn't enough to ease his rigid anger, then nothing is.

"Go back to California, Josie." His voice is rough, serrated. "There's nothing here for you anymore."

"You're wrong." My spine straightens, fresh resolve filling me. "I'm painting the mural. If not on your stupid garden wall, then *somewhere*. Not only did I lose my parents and brother and *you* ten years ago, I lost my sister too. Now the one bright spot in my life is that I'm going to have a nephew. Vanessa and I finally have something to look forward to, and you, of all people, are not taking that away from me." I take a breath and clench my fists. "You once told me you would do anything for me. That all you wanted was for me to be safe and happy. If you really meant that, then *prove it now*."

He grips the doorknob, then stops, his head bowed and shoulders tight. A hard exhale rushes from his lungs. He turns and stalks back to me. Determination glitters in his blue eyes and edges his strong features.

Startled, I step back. Anticipation flares inside me, the strike of a match. He grabs my arms and hauls me against his chest, lowering his mouth to mine in a descent so swift the entire world tilts off balance, and I fall.

CHAPTER 10

Josie

Cole catches me, pinning me against him. And *this* time, the touch of his lips is a thousand things all at once—a shock, a homecoming, an explosion. Fire sparks in my blood. I grip his T-shirt, unable to do anything but kiss him back, our mouths fitting together with such hot, easy pleasure it's impossible to believe that so many years have passed, that we haven't been lovers all this time.

He lifts his palms to the sides of my face, his big hands like a cradle, his thumbs resting in the hollows of my cheekbones. He urges my lips apart with his, and our tongues meet with an electric spark that courses clear down to my toes.

Everything about this—the wall of his chest against mine, the salt-and-citrus scent of him filling my head, the urgent pressure of his mouth, the scratch of his stubble—floods me with relief and pleasure. Thought slips away. Time disappears. It's only me and him again, sinking into the private world only we could ever understand.

He mutters my name under his breath, easing my head back, sliding one hand to caress the nape of my neck. Need uncoils inside me like a bright red ribbon that's been knotted too long.

This is what I've missed, what I've longed for during countless dark nights when my mind is wired with fear and my body aches for comfort. It's him—the way he engulfs me with his entire body, the way we fit together like a lock and key, the way everything bad that has happened or will happen dissolves into the pure certainty of *us*.

I unclench my hand from his shirt and shove it underneath the hem to touch his bare skin. He jerks in reaction, his breath expelling. The sensation of his warm, hard abdomen under my palm floods me with awe and delight.

He's heartbreakingly familiar, yes, but also different. He's harder, older, stronger. My fingers touch the ridge of a scar at his side. He trails his lips to my cheek, his breath hot, his body tensing with an erotic urgency I remember all too well.

He closes his hands on my shoulders and lifts his head, breaking our contact. He stares down at me, his eyes darkened to indigo, a flush cresting his cheekbones. Trembling, I bring a hand to my lips.

The only sound is of our breath. The space between us tightens with thwarted desire and lust.

"I don't want you to get hurt again." The words escape him in a rush. He clenches his fingers on my shoulders. "And if you stay here, you will."

"No." I swallow past the tightness in my throat. "Staying here is my last hope. And if you really don't want me to get hurt again, then stop trying to push me away and act like you don't give a shit about everything we once had. Stop trying to protect me from *you*. It didn't work ten years ago, and it won't work now."

He pushes himself away, his eyes hardening with an internal

battle I've seen before. For a heart-stopping instant, I think he's going to walk out again.

Then his gaze lands on the papers in my open portfolio, the mural images scattered to reveal the drawings beneath.

He freezes.

Panic flickers in my veins. I start forward to close the portfolio. Cole shoots out a hand, bringing me to a halt. He pushes the mural drawings aside and lifts out a torn sketchbook page scrawled with a disembodied head, eyes empty sockets of bright red, skinless lips peeled back in a silent scream.

He stares at the horrific image before lifting his gaze to mine. A cold shudder courses through me.

"It's...um, a preliminary sketch for my last series." With a trembling hand, I push a lock of hair away from my face. *"Distortion."*

Cole's throat works with a swallow. "What happened to the forests full of treehouses and fireflies? The girls lighting their path with candles? The rabbits and badgers?"

I rub my palms on my jeans, hating this further evidence of how much I've changed. "Those are all gone."

His mouth tightening, Cole drops the sketch and looks through the others—gaping mouths, cavernous eyes, skeletal cheekbones dripping with blood.

"Tell me," he demands.

"It doesn't matter, Cole."

"Tell me, dammit." He tosses the images down.

"I...I draw and paint these when I can't sleep." I shove the drawings back into the portfolio, locking them up again. "I guess in some ways it's good because it built my career. People love this kind of art. The first series of paintings I sold through a gallery was called *Dreamland*, six dystopian landscapes of ruined buildings and creatures who are half-human and half-insect. Fucking creepy stuff. They sold almost immediately and the gallery owner asked for more. Soon other collectors and gallery owners were calling. It's almost all I've done for the past decade."

"You've been creating that art for ten years?"

"It's what drove me back here." I clench my shaking hands together. "My nightmares have been getting worse. Last month, I had a solo exhibition of paintings of these decapitated heads. After every painting sold, I had a panic attack that they were still *out there* and would forever haunt me.

"Then I found a painting in my studio that I barely remember creating. It was of a boy wearing a suit like the one Teddy had been wearing the night of the accident, but he had no face. I think I'd done it in the middle of the night. I must have been totally zoned out. It was so weird, like I'd wanted to paint Teddy but I couldn't remember his face.

"And then I got scared, wondering if I really was forgetting him. As if the black hole in my memory was getting bigger and starting to pull other things into it. Even my little brother."

I hug my arms around myself. I've never told anyone all that before. It shouldn't surprise me that it was easy to tell Cole. I used to tell him everything.

He doesn't move. His darkened eyes pin me to the spot. Pressure builds, like the inside of a balloon about to burst.

"It's okay." I swallow to ease my dry throat. "I mean…it's fucked-up and awful and ultimately the reason I'm here, but—"

"You can paint the mural." His voice rasps out of his throat like sandpaper. "I'll tell Allegra tomorrow."

Relief billows through me but doesn't eradicate my despair over the pain this is causing *him*.

"Cole, I'm…I don't want you to blame yourself."

"Christ, Josie." An old, hard agony contorts his features. "There's no one to blame *but* me. *I'm* the fucking reason this happened to you."

Tears burn my eyes. "I never thought of you like that. I meant it when I said I didn't blame you. I hate that so many people still think it was your fault. Even when you left, I knew there was nothing you could have done. If nothing else, I wish I'd told you that sooner."

Our gazes lock like a chain. Raw energy flickers in the air. My pulse increases, driving the despair from my blood and replacing it with a heat I haven't felt in longer than I care to remember.

He opens his palms, unclenching his fists, and takes a step in my direction. The tension snaps. And then we're both closing the distance between each other as if crushing time itself. He spreads his arms out. A cry breaks loose from my throat. Our bodies collide.

I wrap my arms around his neck. He grips the back of my head, his eyes blazing with a sudden naked longing that inflames all my senses. He brings my mouth to his again, a hot open kiss simmering with pent-up lust.

"Cole." I drive my hands into his thick hair. "I *missed* you."

He murmurs my name, locking one arm around my back and lifting me off the floor. Two steps to the bed, and he lowers me onto the mattress, his breath heating my cheek. He stares at me for a second, almost as if he can't believe I'm real.

Knowing he'll think way too hard about this if given a chance, I grab the front of his T-shirt and pull him on top of me, lifting my head to kiss him.

Heat explodes in my chest. And again, this is exactly what I've wanted in those nights when terror splinters my dreams and loneliness weights my soul. I've ached for the strength of him on top of me, his hands buried in my hair, our lips clinging. I've wanted so desperately for the *truth of us* to conquer the horror of what happened to us.

Pressing my hand to his heart, I part my lips for him. He's still the only man in the world who knows exactly how to kiss me. My body softens, heat melting through my veins, a pulse sparking to life in my core. Beneath my hand, his heartbeat quickens, and his muscles tense with the onset of a desire I'd once known so well. Even all these years later, I sense his breath change in rhythm, the urgency already uncoiling in him.

He trails his lips across my cheek and down to my neck, flicking his tongue into the hot hollow of my throat. *God.* It's been so long since I've felt anything like this, the flare of excitement, the sheer pleasure of kissing and being kissed. He tips my chin up and reclaims my lips, sweeping his tongue into my mouth in an act of pure possession.

My heart jolts. He's already getting hard, the thick bulge in his jeans pressing against my thigh. I clench my thighs against the growing ache and lose myself in the heat of our kiss.

After edging his hand between our bodies, he cups my breast, flicking his thumb over my tight nipple.

"I can't wait for you." He lifts his head, his blue eyes smoldering. "I need to see you."

I pull away from him only long enough to yank my T-shirt over my head. A groan of appreciation escapes him at the sight of my breasts cupped in a plain blue bra, my stiff nipples visible through the thin fabric. I'm hot, prickly, excited, and nervous all at the same time. And when he unhooks my bra with one swift twist of his fingers, I arch toward him in invitation.

"Goddamn, Josie." He slides his hand down my belly, pressing his lips to my bare breasts. "Still the most perfect woman ever."

He lavishes kisses over my breasts until I start to pant, my insides twisting with growing pressure. He still knows everything I like, everything I want. Moving down my body, he unfastens my jeans and tugs them off. As he reveals my pink hipsters printed with little bananas, he gives a hoarse chuckle.

"Your underwear was one of the many thousands of reasons I loved undressing you." He presses his lips down my abdomen. "Always a surprise."

He flicks his tongue out to stroke along the edge of my panties. Flames lick through my blood. I drive my hand into his hair, part of me still astonished that this is happening. He hooks his fingers into my panties and eases them down my thighs. Then I'm naked, cooler air brushing over my skin, and a sudden self-consciousness seizes me.

He pauses, his hand on my thigh. "Okay?"

I nod and gulp air into my tight lungs. *More than okay.*

A frown tugs at his mouth. "I don't have a condom, but—"

"It's okay. I'm on the pill for my period, but I haven't had sex in well over a year."

"You need to know I'm healthy." An emotion resembling regret tightens his jaw. "I haven't been celibate, but I've always been safe."

"I know. I trust you." I stroke his stubble-coated jaw and brush my finger over his lower lip. He kisses my palm, then trails his lips over my arm, my shoulder, and back down to my breasts.

Though I'm aching to see him naked, I can't move beneath the exquisite sensations, the haze of lust descending over us. He eases his hand between my thighs, spreading them apart and trailing his fingers up to my sex. He slips one finger into me, a light teasing tickle as if he's letting me get reacquainted with his touch.

But I don't need to be reacquainted with him. His touch, his scent, the scrape of his stubble against my breasts...everything about him is imprinted in the deepest part of my memory. I pull at the front of his T-shirt.

"Take off your clothes."

He moves away to strip off his shirt. Pushing to my elbows, I stare in awe at his naked chest, the perfect slopes of his pecs leading down to an abdomen so well-defined it might have been sculpted by a master artist. His jeans ride low enough on his hips to reveal the V-line of muscles arrowing on either side of his lower abs, and his arms ripple with sinew.

Ten years ago, he'd had a strong, strapping body I'd loved wildly, but *now*...it's like he's set out to rival a Michelangelo sculpture. Like he's *surpassed* one.

"You, uh..." I lick my lips. "You've been working out."

He flicks open the buttons on his jeans. "Sometimes."

"You're incredibly beautiful."

Though he smiles, darkness flashes behind the lust in his eyes. My heart hitches. Then he lowers his head to kiss me again, and my brief unease burns away. Sinking into his kiss, I press my hand to his erection.

"I don't want to wait much longer," I whisper against his mouth.

"Neither do I." He lifts away from me again to take off his jeans and boxers. I close my fingers around his shaft, so long and deliciously thick my entire body zings with anticipation at the thought of having him inside me.

A groan escapes him. He fists a hand in my hair. "I need you."

I never stopped needing you. The confession collects in my throat and stops.

I stretch out on my back. He climbs over me, placing his hands on either side of my head. For an instant, we stare at each other, the air charged with tension, our past, a thousand questions. He lowers his head at the exact same time I lift mine, and all uncertainty falls away under the power of our kiss.

I spread my legs, my heart hammering. My nerves fire to the breaking point. Pressure curls in my lower body. Bracing one hand on the mattress, he positions himself between my legs and eases into me.

God in heaven. Sweat trickles down my neck. I grip his biceps, forcing myself to spread my legs farther. My muscles tighten and loosen at the same time as my arousal rises in increments.

"Open wider," he whispers hoarsely. "Let me in, Josie Bird."

With a gasp, I lift my legs, hugging them tight against his hips. Our skin rubs together, both familiar and new, his chest teasing my nipples so intensely that I swear I could come from the stimulation alone.

But I won't. I want to come with him locked deep inside me. Sliding my hands to his shoulders, I lift my hips to meet him. He pushes fully into me with well-oiled ease, fisting the bed covers beside me.

And then we're united again in the most primal of ways. He pulls back, pushes forward, setting the rhythm that belonged to us alone. I fall back into the tide, the rocking of our bodies, as time slips away and we're Josie and Cole again, tucked away in our shoebox apartment and bound by the shared belief that we'll never be apart.

Words dissolve into grunts, panting, my incoherent pleas for more. He drives into me again and again, urging me toward the pinnacle, his face sweaty and set with self-restraint.

I come with a scream, digging my fingernails into his shoulders, my whole body electrified with sensation. Only when I'm easing down the other side does he thrust again, so hard I feel him all the way to my belly. Burying his head in my shoulder, he shoots deep inside me. His groan vibrates against my skin and echoes clear down to my bones.

When he rolls off me, his chest heaving, I ease on to my side instinctively, the way I always did before. He folds his arm around me and pulls me against him the way he always did before. We lie together in sated silence, our breath easing, the sweat cooling on our flushed skin, my leg spread over his.

The way we always did before.

CHAPTER 11

Cole

I'm a fucking idiot. All I needed to do was stay away from her. Instead, one touch of her cherry-sweet mouth, and all my resolutions went up in flames.

Forget it. Just tell it to her straight. It was a mistake, you're not getting involved, you're—

"I can hear you thinking." Her voice, the bell-like clarity of it hoarsened with a sleepy rasp, slides into my blood.

—a complete asshole if you think you can stay away from her now.

I turn from the dark window where I've been staring at nothing for the past hour.

Damn.

Sleep-rumpled and still flushed, she's tangled in the sheets, her arms wrapped around a pillow. Her green eyes are wary, the skin of her shoulders and neck abraded by red marks. I was too rough with her, too greedy. Still couldn't get enough of her. That will never change.

A struggle knots my chest. I can't get past this fog of...whatever it is. Can't pull my senses out of the past.

The Sunday mornings when I didn't have to work and could lie tangled in the sheets with Josie's soft, warm body tucked against mine. Her hair spread out on my chest, her breath puffing against my shoulder. Lemongrass and cherries. Stroking my hand down her smooth back, squeezing her perfect ass. Her little murmurs and sighs. Another round of sex before I'd get up to make coffee and we'd spend the next few hours lazing around.

Christ in heaven. What I wouldn't fucking give to have that back.

At the very least, I want to haul her close again, drink in her scent, stroke her messy hair back from her face. But that intense urge still wars with eternal knowledge that I shouldn't be around her. Not anymore.

Silence stretches.

"So are you at least going to make me coffee?" she finally asks.

"It's almost midnight." I rub my hands over my jeans, my fingers flexing with my need to touch her. "Did you sleep?"

"A little." She fumbles in the sheets and grabs my T-shirt, slipping it over her head. "That's probably it for the night, though."

"You must be exhausted during the day."

"Yeah. I drink a lot of coffee."

I frown, disliking the idea of her running on caffeine and almost no sleep. "What have you tried?"

"Everything." She pushes her feet into a pair of fuzzy slippers and walks to the kitchen. The T-shirt slides off her shoulder, exposing her creamy skin. "Medications, therapy, counting sheep. When I can get my brain to shut off, I fall asleep pretty easily but then I can't *stay* asleep. And the nightmares freak me out enough that I don't want to go back to sleep even though I'm exhausted."

I look at the window again. How many times has she been scared awake with nightmares of...what? Freakish disembodied, bloody heads? *What the fuck?*

Part of me doesn't want to know what other images are

cutting through Josie's beautiful mind. Another part of me needs to know everything, as if I can plunge in and rip them all apart with my bare hands.

She starts the coffeemaker and returns to sit on the sofa, reaching for a bag of Jolly Ranchers on the table. She peels one open, flicking her tongue out to pull the candy into her mouth. Heat rushes through me.

Attempting to suppress it, I ask, "When did the insomnia start?"

"Couple of years after the accident." She pulls the shirt over her knees. "First I was just scared of the dark. Then I guess my brain connected that fear with the fact that it's dark when I sleep, which led to the insomnia. It's somehow related to two things. The darkness the night of the accident, and the black hole in my memory."

"You still don't remember anything?"

She shakes her head, her mouth thinning. "Only the end of the party."

I remember too much. Everything about that night still snarls, red and scorching, through every part of me. The paralyzing terror. The surrealness and disbelief—that there had been a mistake, this wasn't real, couldn't be happening.

The freezing ocean water seeping under the doors. The shattered windshield. The unnatural angle of Teddy's neck. Instinct taking over—*get out of the car, save her, call 911. God, please... Josie, don't die.*

And stupid details. The mustard stain on the shirt of the interrogating police chief. The fleeting thought that Benjamin and Faith were going to miss their flight to Heathrow. The pen the nurse used, a black ballpoint printed with *Don Smith Real Estate.*

I force my voice to stay even. "What about the nightmares?"

"They're just a mess of spooky stuff. I put them all in my art."

Anger clenches my jaw.

I hadn't known anything about the trajectory of her artwork. I'd fought the urge to find out countless times, stopping myself from hitting the enter key on a search engine even after I'd typed in her name.

My burning need to know how she was, what she was doing, if she was happy, had been appeased only when Gerald mentioned her. *Josie Mays? She's out in California, doing great. Heard she has an art show coming up. She deserves success.*

Which is exactly why I'd stayed the fuck out of it. A good thing, too. If I'd discovered her art sprang from nightmares, I'd have gone batshit crazy. And then barged into her life trying to save her, even though the only way I could do that was by staying far away from her.

Before the accident, her artwork hadn't been all sunshine and roses. She'd been inspired by fairy tales and driven by subversion. Her paintings had been detailed, fantastical landscapes—forests with human-like trees, gnarled riverbanks, swirling sea floors—dominated by resolute heroines making their way through the maze-like lands. Anthropomorphic creatures—foxes in plaid waistcoats, birds wearing monocles—aided the girls on their journeys.

Once upon a time, Josie's work had been about bravery, facing the unknown with courage, finding help where you least expected it.

I let out a long breath. Now that I've crossed the line I swore I wouldn't even go near, all my real urges, the ones I've fought so hard to bury deep, come clawing to the surface.

Protect her. Make her happy. Give her everything. Love her.

With effort, I struggle to shove it all back down, smother it. None of that will ever come to any good.

I don't know what will.

"Cole."

Kryptonite, the way she says my name in that voice. Soft, faintly amused, gentle. Whenever she'd used that tone, I was a heartbeat away from falling to my knees and doing whatever she asked.

That hasn't changed either.

She pushes off the sofa and approaches. I steel myself against her potent effect and silently will her not to touch me.

"You're going to get a headache from all your thinking." She rests her hand on my bare chest.

The heat of her palm burns. She smells like sex. Her lips are reddened, slightly swollen. I want to pull her hair back, tilt her head up, and devour her sweet mouth all over again.

"I know I said I'd hate you for the rest of my life," she says, "but I don't want to."

Her green eyes are luminous. I lost myself in them years ago. If I let that happen again now, I'll never come out again.

"I can't." She moves her hand down my chest, her fingers tracing my abs. "Hate is poison."

"I could…" I swallow reflexively. "I could never hate you."

A faint smile curves her mouth. She lifts her other hand to my hair, twisting a few strands around her fingers. "I've thought about you a lot. I tried not to…tried *hard* not to…but sometimes when I haven't been able to sleep, you've found your way into my thoughts."

"One of my favorite places."

Her smile widens, and a dimple pops into her left cheek. My defenses, what's left of them anyway, crumble. She leans forward and kisses me between the eyes. Slides her lips down to my nose. A soft kiss on each cheek. My chin. By the time she reaches my mouth, my heart is pounding. She straddles my thighs and curves one hand around my nape. Her lips are as soft as a flower petal.

How in the love of God can I let her go again?

She straddles my lap and sweeps her tongue into my mouth, passing me the sticky candy. I should stop this, tell her it was a mistake, but there's no fucking way I can withstand the onslaught of everything *Josie*. I couldn't do it when I was twenty-two. I'm even more powerless now.

She trails her lips from my mouth to my neck, licking the pulse pounding in the hollow of my throat. My blood heats. The sweet cherry candy melts on my tongue.

I settle my hands on her bare thighs and slide them up under the T-shirt. She's so damned *soft*. I always felt like I'd bruise her with my big clumsy hands, callused from hauling up lobster traps.

Now I *want* to bruise her, mark her as mine, leave no doubt that she will always belong to me. Even if I've ruined her.

She shifts back on my thighs, her bare ass warm through my jeans. A little murmur escapes her throat. She's getting hot again.

I pull her back to me, but she resists my grip. Instead she presses kisses down the center of my chest to my abs and licks them one by one. Her breath puffs against my skin. Tension tightens my muscles.

"Josie."

"Stop thinking." She trails her fingers beneath the unfastened buttons of my jeans. I didn't bother putting on my boxers, and when she touches my cock, my whole body jerks to awareness.

She eases off my lap and tugs my jeans off, her eyes darkening with urgency. Kneeling in front of me, she takes my dick in her hand and brings it to her mouth. Every cell in my body goes taut with pleasure.

"Oh, *shit*." I drag air into my lungs and fight for self-control.

Fucking heaven, sinking into her warm wet mouth. Unable to form a word, I grab the front of the shirt and tug sharply. She moves away only long enough to yank the shirt over her head.

The sight of her naked body slams into me like a firestorm. She's all pink and white curves, her nipples quivering, her tits still reddened from my overeager lust. I reach out to grab her breast, desperate to touch her, but she pushes my hand away and lowers her mouth over my shaft again.

Closing my eyes, I rest my head against the back of the chair. She still knows exactly what I love, working her lips and tongue over me with slow, hot strokes. Part of me wants to stay buried in her luscious mouth forever, but there's no way I can withstand the explosive tension.

"Josie." My voice is tight, barely contained.

She eases back, meeting my gaze through the hot air. "Give it to me. All of it."

With a groan, I shove my hips forward. She takes me in again, slackening her throat muscles, letting me thrust as far as I can. My mind goes blank. There's only the heat of her mouth, her hands on my thighs, the pressure building like steam in my groin.

One more thrust and I come. Her eyes widen. She swallows, circling her hand around my shaft and squeezing her eyes shut. She keeps me in her mouth as the pulses ebb, then slowly pulls away with a little moan.

Before she can speak, I haul her up into my lap. She settles her head on my chest, her body a warm, soft bundle tucked against mine. I edge my hand between her legs. A few quick strokes, and she comes with a sharp cry, trembling and clenching around my finger.

"Perfect." I kiss her temple. "You are so perfect."

"I'm not." She turns her face into my chest. "But I'm glad you think I am. Because I really don't want you to regret this."

I can't speak past the sudden constriction in my throat. Instead I tighten my arms around her and press my face into her hair.

She's leaving after the Bicentennial Festival. Five more weeks. If I let myself have five weeks of Josie Mays, that will have to be enough to sate my hunger. It *won't*—not even a lifetime of her will do that—but I can lie to myself. Just like I once told myself we were having a summer *fling*.

"Cole." She looks up at me, putting her hand on the side of my face. "Don't regret this."

"I could..." I swallow hard. "I could never regret *you*."

A thousand other things, yes. But Josie...never.

Her green eyes dim. My insides clench. The last thing I want to do is hurt her. But as easy as it is to lie to myself, lying to Josie is a knife in my gut.

"I don't regret *this*." I push her hair away from her damp forehead. "I don't regret you. I never will. I also won't tell you I've changed, that I'm a better man than what you've heard, that I'm worthy of you. No."

I hold up a hand to stop her inevitable protest. Years ago, I'd fought to be worthy of loving and being loved by Josie Mays. For one incredible year, I'd succeeded. I'd not only felt worthy, I'd proven it with my hard work, academic success, the career and grad school opportunities that were opening up to me. I'd started doing that to get away from my father, and I'd worked even harder at it all to create a future for me and Josie.

Yeah, I'd been worthy.

Before.

"I can't give you anything." I rest my hand on her nape, willing her to believe me. "I have a shitload of money, and if you need—"

"You're seriously offering me money after I just gave you a blowjob?" Bitterness edges her voice, and she disengages herself from me. "Nice."

Irritation scrapes my chest. "*No*, that's not what I—"

"I know what you meant." She slips the T-shirt over her head and strides to the kitchen. "It's the opposite of what happened eleven years ago. Back then, you used your lack of money as an excuse for why you couldn't be with me...when all I wanted was *you*. And now you're trying to convince me that money is *all* you have to offer. I didn't believe you then, and I don't believe you now."

"You should." I pull my jeans on, hitching them over my hips. "Some things haven't changed. You hook up with me again, and you'll get dragged into the shit that surrounds Cole Danforth and Invicta Spirits."

"And you think that concerns me one bit?" She pours the coffee with a sharp movement. It sloshes over the side of the mug. "If the past ten years have taught me anything, it's that life is too fucking short and precious to worry about what other people think of my decisions."

My shoulders tense. Josie sets the mug down and presses her fingers to her temples. Her body heaves with a sigh.

"For God's sake, Cole. First we're fighting about the mural, then right when we come to terms with that, we start fighting about us. I didn't come back here to be angry all the time. I don't want to be. Can't we just be *friends* again?"

She lifts her gaze to mine. *Ah, she used to look at me like that all the time. Any second now, she'll give me her warm, bright smile and kiss me goodbye before grabbing her portfolio of enchanted forest art and hurrying off to her drawing class...*

I flex my hands and struggle to maintain some small piece of my guard to block her out. But whatever is left crumbles like sawdust.

"We can..." Something sticks in my throat. "We can be friends."

"Good." A relieved smile crosses her face, the lines on her forehead easing. "I would really like that."

I can't stop myself from approaching her. Curling a lock of her dark hair around my finger, I kiss her between the eyes. Her cherry taste lingers in my mouth. I want more.

No matter how selfish and greedy it makes me, I crave this woman like a drug. I tell myself I have no choice. She's going to stay whether I want her to or not.

I'll keep her close. Now more than ever, it's the only way to protect her.

CHAPTER 12

Josie

If Cole dominated my thoughts before we had sex, now he *consumes* them. He leaves for New York the following day to attend an Invicta whiskey launch event, which gives me some time to deal with the swift intensity of what's happening between us.

Hot sex and tentative friendship. Given how awful things have been, I will happily take both. Not only am I still tingling two days after our night together, but my heart is comforted by the brief glimpses of *my Cole* that appeared through his guard. I saw the boy I once loved in the way he touched my face and stroked my hair, even in the slouched lines of his body as he sat by the window.

And while I'm under no illusions about reviving what we once had, knowing he's still there—even buried deep—cements my belief that returning to Castille was the right thing to do.

For all my pent-up resentment toward him, all the times I've blamed him for not even giving us a chance to heal together, I couldn't have withstood the reality of that golden, sun-soaked boy having been so completely crushed beneath the weight of unbearable loss.

In his absence, I hasten to get the mural preparations underway. I've gotten behind schedule and have a great deal of catching up to do.

"What changed his mind?" Vanessa asks one evening as we start to get Teddy's old room organized for the nursery.

"Not sure." I shrug, keeping my voice nonchalant. Since I'm still coming to terms with this turn of events, I'm not about to divulge it to anyone else. Especially my sister. "I guess he finally realized it was the right thing to do."

If Allegra King and the festival committee wonder about Cole's change of heart regarding the mural, they all have the grace not to ask questions. Instead they spring into action over the next few days to get the wall prepped and primed.

Using a grid system, I plan to transfer my drawings to the wall a section at a time, completing the entire image as a sketch before painting. Based on my accelerated timeline, I'll be finished with the mural several days before the Bicentennial Festival.

After organizing my supplies, I sketch out the mural in acrylic paint, enjoying the meditative process of starting a new piece. It's what I used to love most about art, being able to lose myself in design and color.

As I draw the foreground ocean, people pause to watch me work, to chat, and to ask questions. This is all enormously gratifying. I'm accustomed to working in the solitude of my studio, so interacting with people and talking to them about my art while it's still in progress is both unusual and welcome.

"I like to paint too," says a child's voice one afternoon.

I turn to find a brown-haired little boy of about eight and his mother standing nearby. My heart bumps. He looks a bit like Teddy did at that age.

"What do you like to paint?" I ask.

"Mostly dinosaurs. Sometimes airplanes." He squints at the mural. "You should put an airplane in there somewhere."

"Good idea. Maybe I will." Though I haven't finished the outline, I take a paintbrush from my case and gesture to the ocean floor. "Do you want to add something to it?"

He glances at his mother, who lifts her eyebrows with surprise.

"Are you sure?" she asks me.

"Of course. What color would you like?" I indicate the paint buckets lined up on a dropcloth beside the wall. "These are the ones we're using for the ocean."

The boy squats to study each color before dipping the brush into a dark green. He then carefully paints the outline of a sea-plant.

I glance at his mother. "Would you like to paint one too?"

"Oh no." She gives me a self-deprecating smile and waves her hand. "I'm terrible at art."

"No one is terrible at art." I take a clean paintbrush from my case and hold it out. "And this part of the design is already outlined, so all you have to do is fill in whatever you want."

"Come on, Mom." The boy crouches to paint another plant.

With a hesitant shrug, his mother starts painting an outline on a pufferfish. Several other people stop to watch. I hand out three more paintbrushes and step back to let two teenaged girls and an older man help paint the ocean scene. Their enjoyment in doing something as simple as coloring in a seashell is a pleasure I hadn't expected. Over the years, I've almost forgotten that art can be *fun*.

When the afternoon light starts to dim, I pack up the paint supplies and return to Vanessa's house to continue working on the nursery. The ocean scene on the nursery walls is a more personal, private mural project. One I'm doing for my nephew, and in some ways for my little brother.

"I'm making spaghetti for dinner, if you'd like to stay." Vanessa stops in the doorway and admires the bright blue walls. "That looks great so far."

"I'll give it another coat tomorrow." I climb off the ladder and wipe my hands on a paint rag. "I'm borrowing a projector from the library, so I can project the scene on to the wall before painting it."

"You're so talented." She leans her shoulder against the door-jamb, resting one hand underneath her belly. "Mom would have been really proud of you."

My heart tightens. "Thanks."

"And I'm glad you came back. It means a lot, having you here."

"I wouldn't want to be anywhere else." I place the lid on the paint can. "I have a show in Los Angeles starting on August fifteenth that I need to get to, but if my nephew hasn't made an appearance by then, I'll come back. I really want to be here for the birth."

"I'll tell him to work around your schedule." She smiles and pats her belly. Warmth passes between us.

"Dinner should be ready by the time you're done." She starts back down the stairs when the doorbell rings.

A moment later, Nathan Peterson's voice comes from the foyer. Carrying my paintbrushes, I walk downstairs and lift my eyebrows at the sight of him in cargo shorts and a T-shirt.

"Nathan, what a nice surprise," I remark.

"Hi, Josie." Faint confusion furrows his brow, and he points to the toolbox he's carrying. "Uh, you asked me to drop by and help put the crib together."

Vanessa throws me a suspicious frown.

"Did I?" I shake my head and laugh. "Sorry, I forgot. But now that you're here, the timing is perfect. I told the delivery guys to leave the crib in the nursery, so we won't have to move it later."

"I can go ahead and get started, then." Nathan pauses and glances uncertainly at Vanessa. "I mean, if it's okay with you?"

"Yes, it's fine." She waves toward the stairs. "Thank you, Nathan."

He heads upstairs, and I attempt to divert past my sister to the basement. She grabs my arm and pulls me to a halt.

"Josie, you are not playing matchmaker," she hisses. "I have enough on my mind without needing to add *dating* to the mix."

"Actually, I think dating is exactly what you need," I counter. "But you don't have to date Nathan if you don't want to. What's wrong with just having him as a friend? I think you could use one."

"And what about *you?*" she retorts. "Last time I checked, you weren't exactly tearing up the rug with a big group of besties."

My heart stutters. She's right. I have a lot of acquaintances, but I haven't had too many close friends over the past decade. People tend to shy away from me after learning about my family, and even if they do stick around, I've often been too spacey or exhausted to commit to their invitations to parties, movies, and dinner. And though Cole and I have agreed to be "friends," that's not nearly the same as having a girlfriend or two just to hang out with.

Like my high-school friends. Lucy, Harper, and Emma. They'd rallied around me after the accident but seeing them had been a gut-wrenching reminder of all I'd lost. Though we'd kept in touch occasionally via email after I moved to California, we'd all gotten involved with our own lives and drifted apart.

"I'm sorry." Vanessa loosens her grip on my arm.

"Don't be. You're right. I can't remember the last time I had lunch with a friend. Well, except for you the other day."

Her expression softens. "I know you're worried about me, but I worry about you too. I've seen your art, and after what you told me...I hate that you're still so hurt."

"Okay, I'll make you a deal." I extend my hand, more determined than ever that both of us will learn how to enjoy life again.

"I'll get out there and make a friend *if* you ask Nathan to have coffee with you."

She bites her lip. "Josie, I don't—"

"Coffee, Vanessa," I reiterate. "You don't have to propose marriage."

"But you could give it a shot," Nathan calls from upstairs.

Vanessa's eyes widen. A bubble of laughter bursts from my throat.

My sister pinches my arm and gives me a *"now look what you did"* glare.

"I made it even easier for you." I nudge her toward the stairs. "Go on."

"I'm never going to forgive you for this." Her skin reddening, she starts up the stairs. "You're such a pain. *And* you still dress like a thrift-shop rag doll."

Tossing her hair, she disappears into the nursery. I hurry to clean the paintbrushes and leave the house, unable to stop smiling.

CHAPTER 13

Cole

Multicolored lights flash over the New York nightclub. Half-dressed dancers gyrate to the thump of a heavy bass. Energy charges the air, fueled by the free-flow of Invicta's Mischief Whiskey. Celebrities, athletes, socialites, and influencers maneuver between the dance floor, the bar, and the VIP areas cordoned off by white silk curtains.

The Mischief Whiskey logo shines from the spotlights. A fifteen-foot cubic structure on the opposite side of the room provides a 4D virtual reality experience tour of Invicta Spirits' newly opened distillery in Scotland.

It's crazed, frenetic, and too fucking much. Especially now, when the only place I want to be is with Josie. Anywhere.

Anywhere but here. Though I'd considered asking her to come with me to the launch party, I couldn't stand the thought of her in this mess. Hated the idea of her seeing what a pretentious bastard I've become. Even if I let myself imagine some tiny possi-

bility that we could ever be together again, I'd never leave Invicta.
It's the only thing that's kept me focused on the future instead of
the past.

And no way could I ever drag Josie into it. She belongs in her
mother's cottage, in the woods, with her paints and easel.
Not...*here*.

Or with me.

"Colton!" An elegant blonde in a skintight red dress peers into
the private alcove where I've been sitting most of the night.
Holding court. "I haven't seen you in *ages*."

She slides into the booth beside me. The cloying smell of her
perfume hits my nose.

"You host the most amazing parties." She sidles closer. Her
skin is hot, her smile framed by lips red as blood. She rests her
hand on my thigh. "And the whiskey is so delicious. The mixolo-
gist made me a cocktail with Mischief and chocolate bitters, and
oh my God, it went right to my *blood*. I might need another."

She giggles and glides her hand closer to my groin.

A reporter for one of the buzz websites approaches, face
flushed and eyes bright. "Mr. Danforth, I've never seen anything
like that virtual reality cube. Can you tell me what prompted you
to use it to launch Mischief?"

"I've always kept Invicta Spirits on the cutting edge of tech-
nology, both in marketing and production." I make an effort to
put some enthusiasm into my voice. "Augmented reality is a
fantastic tool to connect with consumers and allow them to fully
experience the story of our company."

"Awesome, thanks." He puts that quote into his phone and
asks a few more questions before heading back toward the bar,
where the mixologists have been making cocktails nonstop.

"Are you leaving soon?" The blonde settles her hand directly
on my dick, which fails to respond in any way whatsoever. "Want
to give me a ride? Or I could give you one."

Subtle.

I grab her wrist, tightening my fingers unnecessarily hard.

Her eyes widen. "Wow, sorry."

Loosening my grip, I take a breath. Josie's voice echoes in my head.

All I wanted was you.

Eleven years ago, she hadn't cared about my lack of money. Now, she doesn't care about how much I have. Nothing about Invicta—not the company's prestige and success, the expansion, the products, the parties—matters to Josie. All that girl ever cared about was me.

"I gotta go." I edge out of the booth. "Get yourself another drink."

Disappointment flares in the blonde's eyes. "But..."

I signal to my manager that I'm leaving. He nods, swiftly making his way toward the front of the club. Pulling on my suit jacket, I maneuver through the glittering crowd, pausing only to briefly shake hands, respond to a compliment, deflect female attention.

Outside, the night air is a welcome relief. The crowd of onlookers and paparazzi straining at the security barriers is not. They're all holding Invicta swag—hats, bandannas, LED lights. Gerald, who prefers to spend these events working rather than having a good time, is standing near the entrance. He catches my eye and nods to the onlookers.

Tension lines my jaw, but I make my way over to shake a few hands and thank people for their interest in Invicta's latest product. When the valet pulls up with my Porsche, I make insincere apologies and get the hell out of there.

I ease into the Manhattan traffic and return to the penthouse at the SoHo Grand. An exterior landscaped terrace overlooks the city. Loosening my tie, I head outside.

Better. The city is all lights and glitter, but up here it's quiet. The lights illuminate a dizzying drop to the street below.

I lean my elbows on the railing and pull out my cell to call

Josie. Her phone goes to voicemail. My spine tightens. It's not yet midnight. I call again. No answer.

Unease scrapes my chest. What if she's stuck again in the dark? Though she has plenty of flashlights now, she still has to climb the hill to the cottage. And if she panics...

Idiot. She's fine. You're the obsessed fucker who's never been able to get her out of your head.

Not that it matters. She'll be gone in a little over a month. You might never see her again. So you go ahead and store up those thoughts like a fucking dragon hoarding gold because once she's gone, that's it. Done.

My heart pounds. She's under my skin. Inside me. Her cherry taste, sweet soft body, skin like cream. All the parts of her that I broke. Her shattered sleep and terrorized psyche. Her perfect, pure heart. Her belief that hope still exists. That she'll find it again.

I call her twice more. Finally she responds, and the sound of her voice is like fresh water pouring down my parched throat.

"Sorry, my phone was off," she says. "How did the launch thing go?"

I unclench my fist from the railing and take a breath. "It was loud and obnoxious."

"Ah, then you fit right in."

I laugh. "What'd you do today?"

"Trespassed on your property and vandalized your garden wall with an utterly brilliant mural."

"I approve."

"Thank you again for letting me do this. Given that the wall is right outside your office window, I know it's not easy for you."

"Making you happy is always easy." It's the truest statement I've ever spoken.

Well. The second truest.

"Oh." Her voice softens with tenderness. "Even now?"

"Especially now."

The real confession pushes up inside my chest. Smothering it, I grip the phone tighter. "Tell me how it's going."

She starts talking about the priming and outlining, and a little boy and his mother who painted sea plants.

I let her voice wash over the burn inside me, the fire that won't go out, the festering agony that started the second I walked out of her hospital room and tried to convince myself I was doing the right thing.

"You still there?" she asks after a brief silence.

"I'm here."

I'll always be here. But I can never tell her that not for one second in the past eleven years have I stopped loving her.

CHAPTER 14

Josie

After four days of steady work, I start to catch up with the timeline I'd established to complete the mural. I arrive early in the morning, so I can get a few hours of work in alone before an audience starts to gather. The time allows me to prepare for more painters and to ensure the design is still consistent with my plan and color scheme.

As I open a fresh can of paint, a shadow falls over me. I glance up. Cole is standing nearby, gorgeous in a charcoal-gray suit and striped tie, his thick hair combed back from his forehead. Though I still have a hard time reconciling this vision of corporate fortitude with the rumpled boy who'd make me pancakes on Sunday morning, my body lights up with excitement.

"Hi," I breathe. "I didn't know you were back."

"Got in early." He steps toward me, skimming his warm gaze over my paint-splattered overalls and the bandanna covering my hair. "You look good."

Pleasure tingles through me. I want to fly right into his arms, but neither of us moves to touch the other. Pedestrians are walking past us, the square is crowded with people...and since Cole and I are still figuring out how to navigate this new space together, there's no need to draw attention to us.

But oh, how I want him to kiss me.

"So do you." Suppressing a rush of desire, I indicate the mural. "What do you think?"

"It looks great. You've gotten a lot done in the past week. You work all day?"

"Until about three or four, and with a few breaks in between."

"When's your next break?"

I glance at my watch. "Probably around ten."

"Come to my office." He steps toward me, his gaze slipping to my lips. His eyes darken. "I can't wait to kiss you."

Heat blooms through my chest. I nod in agreement. He winks at me and turns to stride into his office. Tempted though I am to follow him, I force myself to wait. At three minutes to ten, I hurry into the inn. The security guard waves me to the stairs without looking up.

Cole is waiting for me at the office door, his beautiful mouth curving with a smile, his eyes crinkling. He holds out his arms. I break into a run and leap right into them. Our lips meet, hot and hard. Our bodies press together. My heart spins like a Ferris wheel, multicolored lights twinkling against the night sky.

❧

Life eases into a welcome routine over the next few days. Morning yoga in the sunroom, coffee and toast, and I'm off to Lantern Square. I work on the mural for most of the day, pausing often to chat with passersby. I feel my parents' pride and enjoyment about the project, and the excitement of the visitors fuels my energy.

"Can I paint one of the Nemos?" A little girl with blonde pigtails stops beside me and points to the outlined school of clownfish.

"Of course." I take a clean paintbrush out of my case and hand it to her. "Paints are right over there."

Two students from Ford's College arrive to paint a shark, and a lobster fisherman stops by specifically to paint one of the half-dozen lobsters I've drawn on the ocean floor. Every day, a crowd has gathered to both watch and help, though I've had to limit the painters to five at a time to allow them room to work.

Aside from requesting that they stick to my established color scheme so the final mural doesn't end up discordant, I let them have at it. Though I hadn't expected people to *want* to paint the mural with me, I'm delighted by both their response and enthusiasm.

In the morning, Cole stops by on his way into the Snapdragon Inn, always bearing the gift of a take-out coffee—large mocha with whip, the kind I'd used to order all the time—and a banana-nut muffin. Also my old favorite. Aside from that gesture, he and I continue to keep our relationship discreet, getting together only in the evenings at Watercolor Cottage.

Though I know Cole is also publicly distancing himself from me to try and protect me from the animosity directed at him, I don't press the issue. Finally we're on reasonably solid ground again, and I'm not about to do anything to change that.

On Wednesday during my lunch break, I stop at the basement archives of Ford College's library. Charlotte the librarian, clad in a gray dress and sweater, welcomes me with the stack of blue-prints and drawings she'd set aside for me.

"I pulled a few more for you, if you'd like to see them," she says.

"No, that's okay. I have everything I need." I pause by her desk, unaccountably nervous. Charlotte is about as timid and nonthreatening a woman as I've ever encountered, and she doesn't seem like the type who would start a friendship with a bunch of personal questions. So...

"There's an exhibition of historical manuscripts over at the museum," I explain hastily. "I wanted to know if you'd be interested in going to see them and maybe grabbing lunch."

She blinks with surprise, like she can't fathom such a thing. "You're asking me to lunch?"

"Yes. I'm not in town for long, but all my friends here have moved away, so I just...um, wanted to know if you'd like to hang out."

A flush crawls up my face. This is nerve-wracking. How do people manage to ask other people out on romantic dates?

"Thanks for the invitation, but actually I...don't really hang out much." She smiles weakly and fidgets with a button on her sweater.

Good lord. She and I are the poster children for Awkward Neurotic Women Needing Social Lives.

"Okay, well, let me know if you change your mind." I grab a notepad from her desk and scribble my cell phone number. "Thanks again for the evil-eye amulet. I think it's working."

"That's good."

As I leave the library, a rush of pity fills me. Does Charlotte spend all her time just working alone in the archives? She can't be much older than me, but she dresses like she's eighty and she seems even more anxious than I am. And that's saying something.

I'll try asking her again later.

"She's kind of like one of your wounded animals, Josie. Maybe you should rescue her." My friend Harper's voice echoes from many years ago. She'd said the same thing about Cole when we'd seen him one night at the pier.

I like to think Cole and I had rescued each other. Maybe we're doing that again now.

Popping a cherry Lifesaver into my mouth, I return to the mural and get to work. At four, when the light starts to change, I clean up the paints and hang a "Back Tomorrow" sign on the scaffolding. I grab a lemonade from a nearby café and sit on a bench to check my phone before making the hike back to Watercolor Cottage.

A large tour bus pulls into the square. Two tour guides descend the bus, followed by a motley group of senior citizens, families, and a couple of college kids. A sign on the bus reads: *Haunted Tours of Eastern Maine.*

Seems more appropriate for October rather than June, but I guess specialty tours are popular year-round. I sip the lemonade, watching the tourists admire and take photos of the Snapdragon Inn.

"Built in 1894, this inn is believed to be haunted by the original owners, Frank and Eleanor Watson," the tour guide calls to the crowd. "Though it's now private property, guests who have stayed at the inn in the past reported sightings of a woman in Victorian clothing climbing the stairs, lights flickering at strange hours, tapping noises, and unexplained footsteps. One guest reported walking into her room and encountering a man wearing a dark suit and hat, who informed her she should return home. Then he turned and vanished into a wall."

The tourists murmur with appropriate awe, cell phones and video cameras clicking.

"If you're interested in a tour, we offer them twice daily during the summer." The second tour guide, a middle-aged man wearing a *Haunted Tours* baseball cap, thrusts a flyer at me. "Tours last five hours and cover all the haunted buildings and sites in the area, including the Stonebridge graveyard."

Out of politeness, I take the flyer and nod my thanks.

"The price includes lunch at the Farmington Lodge, which is haunted by a Civil War soldier," he continues. "Some of our customers have said he's joined them at their table."

"I'll think about it," I promise. "Thanks."

He hurries over to pass out flyers to a couple of women strolling toward the plaza.

Sipping the last of my lemonade, I skim the flyer and start to set it aside when I notice the list of "haunted sites" beneath several pictures of the tour bus, the graveyard, and an old B&B.

Site #12. TRAGEDY AT OLD MILL BRIDGE!

The last stop on our tour, the bridge on Highway 16, is the location of a terrible accident that killed three people. Visitors have heard a woman wailing in the night and seen the ghost of a young boy drifting along the shore of the rocky inlet and crying out for—

Nausea boils into my throat. The plastic cup falls from my cold fingers.

"Josie."

Cole's voice. *God in heaven.*

He's at my side, ripping the flyer from my shaking hand. After scanning the print, he crushes it in his fist and throws it in a garbage can.

"Come with me." He picks up my backpack and grabs my hand, tugging me to my feet.

Blindly I follow him to his office. The instant the door closes behind us, he pulls me into his arms. He's shaking. I press my face to his chest, trying to let the strength of his body, his heartbeat, soothe the shock and panic ricocheting through me.

"What…" I swallow past the tightness in my throat. "What *was* that?"

Before he can answer, a knock sounds at the door. Cole detaches himself from me to open it. An older man stands in the corridor, his features drawn with concern and a glass of water in his hand.

"You okay, Josie?" he asks.

Managing to nod, I sink into a nearby chair. My whole body is still trembling. Cole strides to the window, narrowing his gaze on the tour bus.

The other man hands me the water. Gratefully, I take a swallow, trying to block the image of Teddy's *ghost* wandering along the coastline…

Is that what I've been seeing all this time? The creepy white faces and empty eyes…are my family's ghosts haunting me?

My heart hammers. Lowering the glass, I look at the older man, trying to focus on his face.

"I'm Gerald Parker." He pats my shoulder gently. "Cole's uncle."

"Of course." I wipe a drop of water from my chin. I'd met him only once when Cole and I were together, but Cole had always spoken well of him.

"I'm sorry this happened," he says. "We just saw the bus through the window."

"How…" I pull a breath into my aching lungs. "How long has this been going on?"

"Too long." Cole turns, his eyes hardening. "People have never stopped talking about the accident. By the time I moved back here, that night had already become part of Castille's folklore."

Folklore? The accident that killed three-fifths of my family and destroyed my relationship with the love of my life?

I look at Gerald, as if willing him to refute Cole's statement. Instead he nods somberly.

"They turned the worst, most unimaginable night of both our lives into a *legend*." Cole paces across the room, his back stiff. "And they've kept all the rumors alive, especially the ones about what happened. I was drunk at the wheel. Jealous that you'd been with another guy. I deliberately ran off the road. They know it's all bullshit, but they've been talking about it for a decade."

An ache pushes at the back of my head. I'd known about the rumors, but Vanessa had shielded me from the worst of them. Then I'd moved to California just two months after the accident, needing to get away from everything. Including my sister.

Cole approaches me, his shoulders lined with tension and his eyes dark.

"The tours started shortly after I moved back," he says. "Teenagers still have campfires out there late at night, hoping to see the so-called ghosts. The Seagull Inn got a shitload of press for being the last place your parents were before they died. It makes me sick."

"Cole shut down at least five tour packages over this," Gerald tells me.

"How?"

"Money. He bought them out." Gerald's mouth twists. "But the damned haunted tours are like that whack-a-mole game. They keep popping up."

"The Castille tour companies will never offer them again. I put a stop to that." Cole looks out the window at the bus. "That one is based over in Fernsdown. I guarantee this will be the last time they offer a fucking haunted tour."

Another knock comes at the door, and a slender young man pokes his head in the room. "I've got the budget reports in."

Cole throws his uncle a pointed look. Gerald hurries over to usher the other man out of the room. The door closes.

"I'm sorry." Cole shoves his hands into his pockets, his pained gaze on me. "It's shitty and horrible. I never wanted you to find out."

"Is that why you were trying so hard to make me leave?"

A humorless chuckle escapes him. "One reason. Yeah."

Heavy silence weights the air. I grip the glass in both hands, my insides snarled and tight. My brain can't shake the image of a pale, transparent version of Teddy, still in the suit he'd worn to the anniversary party but without his tie, which he'd taken off less than half an hour after arriving.

It's exactly something I'd paint in one of my insomnia-induced hazes.

What the fuck is happening to me?

"Josie." Faint alarm edges Cole's voice. He settles his hand on the back of my neck. "Lower your head. You look like you're about to faint."

I press my face into my hands. "I can't do this anymore."

"Do what?"

"I'd thought...*hoped*...that coming back would make the nightmares stop. But not only have they not stopped, I'm seeing them in the daytime now. Decapitated heads, red eyes, all the creepy shit in my paintings. Sometimes I feel like I'm going crazy."

Cole's breath escapes in a heavy rush. He kneels in front of me, pulling my hands away from my face. Conviction and something else I can't read burns in his eyes.

"You are *not* going crazy." He tightens his grip on my wrists. "Coming back here after ten years is bound to cause trauma. But you'll heal through all the good you're doing."

With every cell in my body, I want to believe him. But how can I when my mind is still so fractured and dark?

My pulse beats heavily against his fingertips. Cole is the other survivor of that night. No matter what happens with us, we will forever be linked by that horrible connection.

"Why did you warn me about Nathan Peterson?" I ask.

He jerks his head up, wariness discoloring his eyes. "What?"

"When you saw him at the cottage. You gave me a *warning* to stay away from him."

"Because he's no better than his brother."

"That's not true." I shake my head and tug my hands from his. "Nathan is a good guy."

Tension stiffens his spine. He pushes to his feet. "The Petersons and I have enough bad blood without you needing to get in the middle of it."

I frown. "Nathan's father was the police chief the night of the accident. Nathan was there too."

"And?"

"Henry Peterson was the interrogating officer." My unease deepens. "I know you never liked him, but did he say or do anything strange?"

"No." He pulls a hand through his hair and twists his neck. "I mean, he was a cop then, not my father's friend. Far as I know, he handled the investigation well."

"Did you read the police reports?"

"Yeah." He turns back, his forehead creasing. "Why are you asking?"

I rub my aching chest. "Because you're the one who remembers what happened."

"You know what happened. It's all in the reports."

"But we never had a chance to talk about it. Do you ever think about it?"

"Why? So I can go insane wondering what I could have done differently?"

"No." I press my hands to my eyes. "I'm sorry. I don't know what's the matter with me."

"*Nothing* is the matter with you." Cole approaches and bends to press his forehead against mine. "This is why—"

His voice breaks off abruptly. My chest constricts.

—*I wanted you to leave.*

He doesn't have to finish the sentence. Maybe he'd been right all along.

No. If I'd left, we never would have found *us* again. Or rather, this new tentative version of us.

After slipping his hand under my chin, he lifts my face to look at him. Though his eyes are gentle, brackets of tension line his mouth.

"Josie, you've told me so many times you came back to do something good." He strokes his hand over my hair. "I *beg* you not to let this change that for you. Please."

I lean forward and press my forehead against his abdomen. Despite the hallucinations, it's true that I'm beginning to find light here again. And I feel like the same thing is happening for both Cole and Vanessa too.

"I won't." I slip my arms around his waist and hug him. "I'm okay."

"You're extraordinary." He returns my embrace. "Now give me a couple of minutes to get this meeting taken care of. Then I'll take you home."

He kisses the top of my head and leaves. I sink back into the chair, my heart still racing. Drawing in a breath, I catch sight of a large world map pinned to the wall. I hadn't noticed it the last time I was here.

Rising slowly, I walk to the map. The surface is dotted with multicolored pins that clearly indicate businesses or regions Invicta Spirits has a stake in.

But the map's intent matters far less to me than the fact that Cole is using a paper wall map and stick pins to plot his world domination or whatever.

This tangible evidence of the boy I once knew eases the pain in my chest. For a long time, I stare at the map. It had once been so easy to love Cole Danforth. Forcing myself to fall out of love with him had been the hardest thing I've ever done.

But I didn't succeed. Not one bit.

CHAPTER 15

Josie

Though I try to put the haunted tour out of my mind over the next few days, the horrific idea still lingers. I've never had the intention of returning to the accident site. In fact, I've gone out of my way to avoid it. But knowing people are visiting the inlet as a *tourist stop* evokes a strange urge to see it again, as if I can somehow reclaim it.

Highway 16 and the Old Mill Bridge are the only geographical elements in Castille I haven't included in the mural. And though people continue to stop by to help paint—my former art teacher, several of my father's friends, even Allegra King—only Cole knows about the secrets I've hidden in the design. There's the secrets wall, of course, the granite stones beside the lighthouse where visitors leave scraps of paper on which they've written a secret.

All the other secrets are mine and his. There's the silhouette of my father in the post office, and a replica of my mother's

Beatrix painting on the Castille Museum wall. Teddy, wearing his favorite *Star Wars* T-shirt, is playing tetherball amidst a group of children on the school playground.

And there are the secrets Cole and I share—the platform tree-house, the red candy jar in the window of the Sugar Shop, the figures on the carousel.

Maybe someone will look closely enough at the mural to discover my secrets. Maybe not. With the ocean in the fore-ground, the mural is a sweeping panorama of the town's history populated by hundreds of people and scenes, all scaled to the millimeter and set among Castille's famous and ordinary surroundings—downtown buildings, the lighthouse, the lobster shacks, the carnival, the schools and cafés.

Secrets or not, it's everything *good* about this town.

I step back to study the Lantern Square scene, where I've finished painting the courthouse.

"Josie?"

I turn to face a stunningly beautiful woman with auburn hair. She lifts her hand to shade her eyes from the sun.

"I'm sorry I'm interrupting," she says.

"No problem. What can I do for you?"

"My names is Eve Perrin." She gives me a warm smile and extends her hand. "I'm so happy to finally meet you."

I wipe my hand on my overalls, conscious of her elegant silk blouse and pencil skirt, before shaking her hand.

"I'd intended to introduce myself when you first arrived, but unfortunately I've been out of town," she explains. "I've heard so much about you. I'm an art historian, and while my specialty is nineteenth-century art, I've been drawn to the surreal quality of your paintings. Your work is incredible."

"Thanks." A flush rises to my face. Much as I appreciate the compliment, I dislike thinking of my freakishly "surreal" art.

"Do you have another series planned for when you finish the mural?" she asks.

"Not really. I'm hoping to find a new aesthetic, though. Something…lighter."

"I've been working with several art galleries in town." She slips her hand into her pocket and extracts an embossed business card with her name and number. "I'd love to help you set up an exhibition here in Castille, if you're interested. We could organize it as the launch of your new aesthetic."

I'm not sure how to respond. I'd love to relaunch my career in Castille, but I don't know if I'll come up with anything *hopeful* after I finish the mural. Creating the history of Castille is both a catharsis and an academic exercise—I've had to relearn proportions, perspective, and realism, which my weird, creepy nightmare paintings lack entirely.

But after this?

"Thank you," I finally say. "I'd be honored, but honestly, I don't know what I'll paint after the mural."

"There's no hurry at all." She smiles and nods at the business card. "I'm at your service whenever you need me. If you have time, I'd love to take you to lunch and talk about your work. No pressure, though."

"I'd like that too. Thanks."

We make arrangements to stay in contact before she walks toward a nearby café. Not knowing what to make of her overture, I watch her go. I want Castille to know me for the mural, not my horror-show art.

Still, Eve seems nice, and I like the idea of having lunch with her. Maybe if I make *two* friends, I can convince Vanessa to actually kiss Nathan.

I tuck Eve Perrin's card into my backpack and continue working. As evening light descends, Cole comes down from his office to help me pack up the supplies.

"You'll be done with this long before the deadline." He pauses to study the mural. "How many people have worked on it?"

"I don't know. I'm keeping a list, though. Maybe we can

have a plaque made later with the names of all the contribu-
tors." Wiping my hands on a rag, I admire the mural alongside
him. "I hadn't expected it to become a community effort, but I
love that it's turned out that way. Are you going to paint
something?"

"I'll leave that to you and the town's artists." He nods toward
his Porsche, which is parked nearby. "Come home with me."

I indicate my dirty clothes and hands with a grimace. "I'll get
paint all over your leather seats."

"Good." He opens the passenger side door and gives me a
wink. "Then you can get paint all over me."

Oh, Cole Danforth. It's still so easy for you to disarm me.

We get into the car, and a few minutes later he pulls into the
driveway of his oceanfront mansion. The spotlights blaze over
the garden. I haven't been here since the night he rescued me
from the dark.

Despite the magnificence of our surroundings, we slip back
into the past of what we once were. He bakes a frozen pizza, and
we eat at the kitchen counter while discussing *Empire of the Gods*,
a show we'd been binge-watching together in the weeks right
before the accident.

"Did you ever finish the series?" I peel the melted cheese off
my pizza.

"No. Did you?"

"No. I think it lasted for another two years. I wonder what
happened to Lazarus." Tilting my head back, I drop the cheese
into my mouth.

Amusement creases his eyes. "You still eat the topping off
your pizza first?"

"Then the crust." I hold up the sauce-covered crust. "Do you
still eat kids' breakfast cereal? Lucky Charms?"

He shakes his head. "Raisin bran and egg-white omelets."

"Oh my God." I groan with dismay. "You've become such an
adult."

"I even pay my bills on time and eat my vegetables." He shoots me a grin and rises to take our plates to the sink.

I rest my chin in my hand, studying him. "So what *else* do you do? Besides stomp around like Godzilla destroying everything weaker than you."

"What do you mean, what else do I do?" He washes the plates and sets them in the drainer.

"For fun. Do you still swim and visit the aquarium? Do you see every action movie on opening day and go down to Boston for Red Sox games? Do you camp on Eagle Mountain and go fishing?"

"No." He dries his hands on a dishtowel, his forehead creased. "I work. That's why Invicta is so successful. I've put everything I have into it."

"Why distilled spirits? You didn't even like beer, much less liquor."

"I lived in New York for a while." Tossing the towel aside, he leans back against the counter. "Got a job with a hydropower company where my uncle worked. I learned a lot about business, then talked to a guy who'd been thinking about starting a distillery. He asked if I was interested. I wanted something else to do, so I agreed. Turned out I was good at it, so I left to start my own company."

"What about marine biology?"

He shrugs. His eyes cloud over. "Didn't work out."

I straighten and stare at him. A sharp pain fills my chest. Though there's no denying his business success, even after the horror of the accident, this isn't how it was supposed to turn out. How *he* was supposed to turn out.

The Cole of ten years ago—*my Cole*—had ambitions, goals, a map of the future. He'd been determined to work by the ocean with the sun blazing overhead and the salty wind filling his nose. I'd hoped to attend art school at UC Berkeley, and he'd planned to go with me. He'd get a job at an ocean conservation institute or as a lifeguard before applying to graduate school. We'd get married one day, buy a little house…

We'd gotten close enough to that dream to see it as our future. Then everything changed, but I'd still built a life in California for myself. Cole hadn't lived any part of his dreams.

"What about grad school?" I ask.

"Never applied. I didn't finish undergrad."

I press a hand to my chest. "You never graduated?"

His jaw tensing, he pushes away from the counter and starts to fill the coffeemaker.

"But you…you were two weeks away from graduation."

"Things changed."

"I *know*, but…Vanessa told me you didn't leave Castille right away."

"No. I didn't go back to school either."

Guilt pierces me. "Was it because of her lawsuit?"

His breath expels in a sigh. "It was a bunch of shit, Josie. That was just part of it."

"I want you to know I didn't have anything to do with it. I tried to stop her because even though I was so angry with you, I never thought the accident was your fault."

He shakes his head. "It doesn't matter."

"It does matter. I'm sorry she did that. And I never understood why you settled when the police reports had concluded you'd done nothing wrong."

Cole stabs the start button on the coffeemaker and drags a hand down his face. "I gave her the money because I couldn't stand the thought of the accident being replayed in court, and *you* being forced to relive it."

A wave of shock courses through me. "You did it for me?"

"Why else?" His mouth twists with self-deprecation. "After what I'd done, I sure as hell didn't want a lawyer interrogating you about the worst night of your life."

"I...I couldn't have given him many answers. I didn't remember anything."

"I know." Turning away from me, he takes two mugs from the cupboard. "I didn't want to go through it again either. It was easier just to settle."

"But where did all that money come from?" Though I suspect I already know the answer, a sudden fear lights in my heart. "Your father?"

"Some." He sets a mug in front of me, his expression closing off. "The rest was all of my trust fund. I went to work for the Iron Horse to pay it off. That was why I couldn't leave right away."

I close my eyes. "Cole, I'm so sorry. You working for your father was never what I wanted. It must have been awful for you."

"Nothing I hadn't been through before."

Sorrow and regret surge inside me. After shedding the troublemaker label from his childhood, and then being driven back under his father's control...he'd have been forced to endure even more fire from the community.

"I know your father was all upset about the rumors," I say. "It must have gotten worse after the lawsuit."

"Yeah." He rubs a hand over his jaw, a sudden fatigue creasing his features. "When word got out that I'd settled the lawsuit, everyone assumed I was guilty. That I'd gotten away with murder. They still think that."

I can only imagine the gossip. *Cole Danforth was always a problem. Pity, since his father was such a good man. Not surprised he ended up like this. Poor Faith and Ben, mixed up with that boy. If he wasn't drinking, he was on something. Josie should never have had anything to do with him.*

"They can't possibly still think you were at fault." Tension constricts my jaw. "The police reports..."

"No one cares about the police reports." He grabs the coffeepot with a sharp movement and pours coffee into the mugs.

My discomfort intensifies. *I'd* cared about the police reports. They're still the source of my lost memory. The only way I know what happened.

"Josie, it's all over and done with." Cole shoves the pot back onto the burner, his shoulders stiff. "I sure as hell don't want to go back and relive any part of it. And from what you told me, you don't either. You want to look forward, not back."

I nod, though unease shivers through me. Reflexively, I touch the evil-eye amulet I still carry in my pocket. How can I look forward if I'm still haunted by creepy things lurking in the dark? Faces staring at me? What if they never go away?

"Hey." Cole stops in front of me, his big solid presence dispelling my anxiety. He nudges his body between my legs and lowers his head to kiss me. "I can hear you thinking."

A chuckle rises to my throat. "We do a lot of that, huh?"

"Sometimes I think of good things." Running his hand over my hair, he pulls away and picks up a white bakery box from the counter. "Especially this little woodland elf who ended up being the best thing that happened to me."

My heart clenches. "We *were* good, weren't we? Even if I did have to throw myself at you with wild abandon to get you to realize that."

He grins at the reminder of the first time I'd kissed him on the Water's Edge Pier. Even now, I still remember our bodies pressing together, the combined tastes of cherry and pineapple Lifesavers, the urgent way he'd returned my kiss.

"We were very good." He opens the box and removes a white cake elaborately decorated with little yellow leaves and swirls.

Shocked, I stare at the curly writing: *Happy Birthday, Josie Bird.*

"Oh my God." I lift my gaze to his. "It's my *birthday*. Things have been so crazy and…just *weird* that I totally forgot."

"I didn't." Looking rather pleased with himself, he takes two plates from the cupboard. "I still have the party invitation you gave me when you were nine."

"Really?" Pleasure fills me. "That's so sweet."

He puts several candles on the cake and lights them, then sings "Happy Birthday" in a low, warm baritone that sinks right into my blood. Before blowing out the candles, I grab his tie and tug him toward me for a kiss.

"I wish us both peace," I whisper against his lips. *Together.*

Tension rolls through him for an instant. He puts his hand on the back of my neck and deepens the kiss. "Better blow out your candles before they set my tie on fire."

With a smile, I pull away and blow out the candles. He cuts the lemon cake, which is sweet and delicious, but not *quite* as good as the dry, sour lemon cake he'd made for my twentieth birthday.

"Come with me." He takes my hand and tugs me to my feet. "I have a present for you in my bedroom."

"I'll bet you do."

He tosses me a narrow glance. "I mean a *real* present."

"Mmm. A real big one?"

He shakes his head at me and laughs. We walk upstairs to his third-floor bedroom, and the instant I precede him past the door, warmth floods me. Everything in this room reminds me of the boy he'd been.

A computer desk is cluttered with papers, and the cat Curly is stretched out on the rumpled navy comforter. A bookshelf stuffed with paperbacks sits beside the door, a speaker system is attached to the wall, and clothes are scattered around—a hoodie, wrinkled T-shirts, a pair of jeans.

I run my hand over a T-shirt lying on the bed. It's inside-out, and there's a worn spot at the back of the neck. Proof that he still takes off his T-shirts by tugging the back collar rather than pulling up the hem.

"This is where you are."

"Where I am?" He pulls his eyebrows together.

"Your stuff." I indicate the room. "The rest of the house looks like a showroom, but *my* Cole was here all along."

He smiles—a smile exactly like the kind he'd give me when I'd bound into the apartment after a day of classes. A smile that crinkles his eyes at the corners and displays his beautiful white teeth. A smile that says he's happy I'm home, he's glad to see me, he's about to come over and kiss me.

He takes a polka-dotted gift bag from the desk. "Your first present. I'll have another for you in about five minutes."

"That long?" Arching an eyebrow, I take the bag from him.

"Actually, it's a lot longer."

I grin and sit on the bed, enjoying the excited anticipation of opening a present. I open the bag carefully and part the tissue paper. A glimpse of red peeks through.

"What…" I reach in and pull out a red backpack patterned with huge yellow daisies.

My heart stutters. Embroidered above the pocket is the name JOSIE in blue letters. I lift my gaze to Cole in astonishment.

"My *backpack*."

If he was pleased with himself about remembering my birthday, now he looks downright smug. "Your black one is way too boring for you. And I never forgot that red backpack of yours, so I had one made."

"Oh, Cole." A ridiculously powerful rush of emotion squeezes my chest. Tears fill my eyes. "I loved that backpack so much. I can't believe you did this. I can't believe you *remember*."

"I remember everything about you." Tenderness softens his features. He threads his hand through my hair. "That will never change. But you're really not allowed to cry, or I'll think I did the wrong thing."

"No." I wipe my eyes with the back of my hand. "You couldn't have done anything more *right*. Thank you so much."

He presses a kiss to my forehead and hands me a tissue—one

that is thick and infused with lotion. I dab my tears and set the backpack at the foot of the bed.

After getting to my feet, I slide my arms around his waist. He settles his hands on either side of my neck. As we gaze at each other, we both know it's just us again, all our heartache and friendship still binding us inextricably together.

He slips his hand beneath my chin and brings his mouth to mine in a warm, gentle kiss that sparks me with heat. We tumble onto the bed. Curly meows a yelp of outrage and bounds out of the room.

Cole climbs on top of me, his body a big, welcoming weight. I wind my arms around his neck as our mouths open—hot and wet. A thousand sparks flare through me. He makes a muffled noise in the back of his throat and slides his hand up to cup my breast through my oh-so-sexy overalls.

I grab his wrist, stopping his exploration. "Don't you want me to clean up first?"

"Hell, no." He nuzzles his nose against my shoulder. "I like you dirty."

With a laugh, I cup his face and bring his mouth to mine again. We strip slowly, fumbling with my overall buckles and the knot of Cole's tie. I love seeing his strong body revealed bit by bit, and by the time he's down to his boxer briefs, I'm already wet and aching. I rub my hand over the length of his erection pressing against his briefs and along his upper thigh. Shivers of anticipation race through me.

He tugs my overalls and T-shirt off, his breath escaping at the sight of my pink bra and panties patterned with chili peppers. He palms my breasts, massaging my nipples through the cotton before gliding his fingers down my abdomen.

"Tell me," he orders, tracing my bellybutton with his forefinger.

I twitch under him. "Tell you...?"

He gives me a wicked smile. "Tell me what you want."

"Oh…" I swallow to ease my dry throat. "I want…want you to touch me."

"You do, huh?" He slips his fingers under the waistband of my panties. "You're hot under here, aren't you?"

"So hot," I breathe, wiggling my hips in desperation. "Please, Cole."

Instead of heeding my plea, he unclasps my bra and lowers his head to kiss my breasts, flicking his tongue over my nipples, his breath heating my skin. He slides his hand under my panties again, finding the cleft between my thighs.

"Ah, fuck, Josie." He pulls in a hard breath, easing away to tug my panties down my legs.

Butterflies spin and twirl in my belly. He sheds his boxers before kneeling beside me. My hand trembling, I wrap my fingers around his shaft, easily recalling the rhythm he'd once loved. His breathing increases, sawing through the air above me. He's looking at me with a flush of heat cresting his cheekbones and his eyes dark with want.

"Open up, Josie Bird," he murmurs, pressing me back onto the pillows.

I stretch out, my heart pounding wildly, my whole body primed and ready. Cole moves to settle between my legs. He strokes his hand up my thigh, curving his fingers between them, and rakes his hot gaze over my damp skin and bare breasts. I close my eyes, arching upward as I feel him begin to slide into me, inch by delicious inch.

"So fucking good." He lowers his mouth to mine. "Let me all the way in."

Lifting my legs, I wrap them around his thighs and open myself completely. With a grunt, he thrusts fully into me. I gasp, gripping his shoulders, tensing with anticipation for what will come next…

He pulls back and plunges in again, his muscles straining and flexing. Again and again, driving our arousal to the breaking point. My head spins, everything inside me exhilarating in this crazy rush. I bite down on his smooth shoulder, struggling to retain the control slipping from my grasp with every passing second.

"I feel it," I breathe, straining. "I want to...harder...I'm so close, I..."

He surges into me, hitting the sweet spot. A firestorm ignites. Stars burst behind my eyes, submerging me in bliss. Cole thrusts again and stills, surrendering to his own release. A deep groan rumbles from his chest. Still shuddering, I'm unable to take my eyes off him as he crests the wave.

"Ah, fuck, Josie, you're amazing." He rolls to his back with a groan. "So much better than a chocolate factory."

I laugh. Happiness and utter satiation billow inside me. I tuck myself against the solid wall of his body. He rests his arm heavily over my shoulders. His heart is a steady, rhythmic metronome flowing into my ear. A lullaby strong enough to quiet even my overworked brain and damaged soul.

Darkness beckons. Beside the man I never stopped loving, I close my eyes and let myself fall.

CHAPTER 16

Josie

I wake with a start some time later, though without the usual heart palpitations and lingering fear of a nightmare. My pulse is even, and I haven't broken into a sweat. Both nightstand lamps blaze light through the room. Cole is still asleep, the angles of his face softened in repose, his eyelashes like black feathers against his cheekbones.

Pressing a kiss to his bare shoulder, I climb out of bed and tug his T-shirt over my head. It's close to eleven. The red backpack is still at the foot of the bed. For the first time in ages, my heart is *light*. Unclouded. Clear.

I pull on a pair of socks, intending to go to the kitchen for a snack and some sketching. As I walk toward the door, I notice a fuzzy stuffed animal lodged on the lowest shelf of the bookcase.

Is that...?

I bend to tug the animal out. My throat closes over. So worn most of its fur is rubbed off, the rabbit has gray floppy ears, huge blue eyes, and a cottontail that used to be white but is now gray.

Wally.

My old best friend, whom I used to haul around in my backpack all the time when I was a kid. Wally had moved into the apartment I'd shared with Cole, living mostly on my dresser or closet shelf. I'd never thought about what had happened to him.

After I'd been released from the hospital, I'd gone straight to live with Vanessa. She'd hired a moving company to pack up and move my belongings out of the apartment so I wouldn't have to go back. I'd eventually gone through a few of the boxes, but I hadn't thought about Wally.

Cole had taken him. Kept him.

Tenderness softens me. I lean down to put Wally back in his place on the shelf.

My heart suddenly slams against my chest. On the shelf above, there is a framed 5x7 color photograph of me with my parents, Vanessa, and Teddy. It's the picture Cole had taken on the night of the anniversary party, the last photograph of my family all together.

I haven't seen it before. I'd forgotten it even existed as a physical photograph. It's my last memory of that night, this moment just as Cole pressed the shutter button and the bright flash went off.

My throat tight, I straighten and stare at the photo. My parents, Vanessa, and I are standing in a half-circle with Teddy in front of us. He's holding a white bakery box. We're all smiling and tired. I'm behind Teddy, one hand on his shoulder and the other holding the ridiculously large wooden keychain—shaped into a B for Benjamin—that had belonged to our father.

Teddy had made the keychain for him in woodshop, and though it was unwieldy and impractical, our father had immediately attached all his keys to it and carried it everywhere. When he stuffed his keys in his pocket, the wooden letter B would flop against his hip. He didn't care, remarking that he was likely the only person in the world who never lost his car keys. Teddy had been indescribably proud.

I study the picture for a moment longer. A prickling sensation nudges my chest. I move closer to the nightstand and turn the photo toward the light.

The party was winding down. We were getting ready to go home. We had our spring raincoats on. All our goodbyes had been said. We'd had no idea that twenty minutes later, we'd be half-submerged in the ocean, crushed in a mass of twisted metal.

Everything in the picture makes sense—our smiles and happy weariness, the flowers in my mother's arms, Teddy's missing tie, the bakery box that contained leftover cake.

Everything except…

Why am I holding my father's car keys?

ABOUT THE AUTHOR

New York Times & USA Today bestselling author Nina Lane
writes hot, sexy romances about professors, bad boys, candy
makers, and protective alpha males who find themselves
consumed with love for one woman alone. Originally from
California, Nina holds a PhD in Art History and an MA in
Library and Information Studies, which means she loves both
research and organization. She also enjoys traveling and thinks
St. Petersburg, Russia is a city everyone should visit at least once.
Although Nina would go back to college for another degree
because she's that much of a bookworm and a perpetual student,
she now lives the happy life of a full-time writer.

Sign up for Nina's newsletter and receive a free novel!

www.ninalane.com

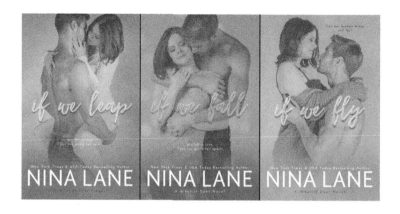

First we fell in love. Then we fell apart.

Shattered by tragedy a decade ago, two lovers fight the secrets that could destroy them.

"This book is a work of art."

A woman fleeing scandal. A town's mysterious recluse.

Lust and secrets collide in this provocative romance.

THE SUGAR RUSH SERIES

Taste the sweetness of life.

From the Stone family patriarch down to the youngest bad boy, follow the lives and loves of the Sugar Rush men in Nina's sexy, compelling series.

THE SPIRAL OF BLISS SERIES

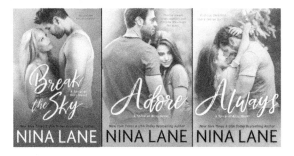

"Give me a kiss, beauty."

From an exhilarating crush to the intensities of marriage, Liv and Dean West embark on a passionate lifelong journey together. As the medieval history professor and his beloved wife face both personal challenges and painful battles, they never lose sight of the hope, humor, and devotion that belong only to them.

Liv and Dean's everlasting romance will melt your heart, turn you on, and enchant you with the power of a love to end all loves.

Printed in Great Britain
by Amazon